THE DESIDERIOS

(BALAVAN BOOK ONE)

SYLVIA S. LEE

MEGAN H. LEE

Prologue

A man stands at the front of the war, the symbol of the Legion, their pride. He is their statue to lead the way.

But as he stands there, as he watches the young people die, like flies, he is not the cold-hearted man people expect him to be.

He is, perhaps, not even a full man himself, but more a boy to be precise. A mere boy with the largest weight on his shoulders possible.

He stands on the battlefield and watches as soldiers clash against one another, a child fighting another soldier. Slitting each others' throats in order to live another day.

As the war dragged on, more and more people were drafted into the ranks, and soon the age limit became younger and younger.

Some of them are almost a decade younger than him.

But as time goes on, and the battle is no longer anything but dead bodies and a blood run battlefield, he turns away. It is not his duty to clean up afterwards.

He would fight and fight, but to what end?

So he leaves the cries for help and the rushing nurses and medics behind.

He enters his tent with a sigh and lies down on his cot. His mind slowly drifting away as he falls into a deep sleep with only one last thought clawing its way to the surface.

Who will save us?

Chapter 1: The Legion

Smoke flows in the air, covering almost the entire battlefield. The smell of sweat and death is overwhelming. Above all, one sound rings above all the others in a constant barrage. A shoot rings out across the battlefield. Two more follow. All three of them hit their target. The man falls to the ground in pain, letting out a cry of anguish. His knees buckle as he lurches back and forth in agony. On the other side of the battlefield, the shooters hoot and laugh with exhilaration.

They have finally done it! They've got him! All three snipers pat each other in the back for a job well done. In their haste in celebrating, they assume that the man is dead and fail to notice that he has stood right back up, as if nothing has even happened, despite three distinct streams of blood flowing out of his body, covering his entire body in dark red liquid. The laughing and shouting end immediately. When one of them falls silently to the ground, the others whip around just in time to see the face of their executioner. None has the time to fight back before they hit the ground lifelessly.

The man is there, with three bullets firmly lodged in his chest as blood pours out of each wound. All that can be heard are cries of pain as the rest of platoon is destroyed. The smell of blood wafts in the air. There is now only one man still standing.

*

A large, regal building stands in the middle of a field of obstacle courses and barbed wires. Around it lays no life, nothing but an empty field and dead wildlife caught in traps. Mud surrounds the building and is filled with detonators all

1

around the perimeter – a picturesque view of the Legion headquarters.

A lone truck comes through the fence. It pauses in front of the entrance for a minute to be authorized before moving on.

A nervous figure is dropped out of the truck and makes his way into the building. He is young, fairly short and the perfect image of an anxious man.

The entrance is deathly quiet, with only soldiers standing guard, as silent as statues themselves. The young man nervously slides by them as he enters the dark headquarters as silently as he can. The emptiness causes the little sound he makes to be magnified in the grand opening hall.

It does not seem that he is quiet enough when a hand suddenly claps over his shoulder, emitting a loud echo around them. He jumps almost a foot in the air from fright and turns in time to glimpse the figure standing behind him. Seeing who it is, he lets out a small sigh of relief.

A chuckle rings out and the familiar figure speaks. "Well, Newbie! How's it going? Have you found out where you are supposed to be meeting now?"

"What do you mean?" Max looks at him in confusion.

He just got here about five minutes ago, and he is supposed to know where he needs to be heading already?

This odd man is Thom, his old friend who introduced him to Legion, and he was inducted just a week ago before coming here.

*

The Legion is a formidable force. They are the government's only sanctioned form of military in Balavan. They have full authority to raise arms against any enemy who may be a threat to them – no questions asked. They can also arrest and shoot anyone they suspect to be an enemy. Hence, when a person disappears off the streets or bodies are found floating in rivers, no one dares to ask.

Balavan has long been an autonomous dominion for as long as anyone can remember. Being the largest realm on an island that is the size of a small continent, the people governing it have always considered themselves to be the rulers of everyone on it. Even though there are many natural resources on this island, there are few attacks from the outside world because of its distance from other people. Of course, that does not mean that everything is peaceful or even blissful.

On the contrary, there have been many wars during its long history. All of which are conflicts against their own men or their neighbors.

An elected official is given the title of Sovereign. This individual has the privilege of ruling Balavan and overseeing everything that goes on, including the Legion. The man in charge today goes by the name of David Carson, a weak man who was elected because he agreed to everything that anyone asked even if they were in conflict with a promise that he already made to another constituent. He was also not beyond accepting bribes. In the event that a conflict does occur, he would favor the party that has given him the most monetary incentive.

Of course, his most lucrative clients are members of the Legion who have long been considered the elite members of the realm. Because of the great power and responsibilities that comes along with the job, it is a great honor to be a part of the Legion. It also comes with a great deal of perks. In addition to the outrageous high pay, the legionnaires receive many luxuries that are far out of range for even the highest standing civilian.

*

Thom smiles at the confused recruit and grabs his arm. He drags him down the hall while he struggles to get back on his feet. All the while, Thom is laughing at him. Amidst the dark and confusing halls, they reach a large brown door that looks just like the last hundred identical doors that they have already come across while he is being dragged.

Thom, being the dramatic one, throws open the doors with a loud bang and yells out their arrival.

"I found the Newbie!"

The room is filled with a large wood table and six very hard, uncomfortable looking chairs that look very professional. To Max's confusion, however, no one is sitting there at all. They are all standing around and chatting amongst themselves. It was very casual for such a stiff looking place.

He opens his mouth to say something when Thom suddenly shouts, "Hey! Pay attention to your acting officer!" His tone has rapidly changed from playful to commanding. Instantly, all of the officers stand to attention and salute him.

Max looks up at Thom just in time to see him wink at him. The other officers are about to sit down in the uncomfortable chairs when Thom waves them all away.

"No, no, don't sit there. I don't want to have to sit and have my butt be sore later on."

Again, he is back to normal. He was always an oddball, that one. Max glances at everybody in the room. Some of them are very high commanding officers. He wonders how much power Thom has in the Legion. All he knows is that Thom is his childhood friend, and he hasn't seen him since they were picked for the Legion to fight against the guerrillas.

Because Max was fairly short and scrawny, he initially did not qualify for military service and was quite glad when he was passed over. Thom, though, has always been the golden hero who is kind and popular with everyone. The recruiters selected him immediately as soon as they saw him.

It's been five years, and they have both grown up quite a bit since then. Even though Max is still his little self, he has become the best sharp shooter in the east, which he has proven by winning championships three year in a row – a feat that has not been bested before or since.

Thom found him and picked him up as soon as he could. Max still didn't know anything about his role in the Legion, though.

He finds out quickly, however, when the others start to address Thom.

"General Thomas, we have been waiting for you to come. There is some urgent news that you need to—"

Max finds it strange that the man refers to his friend in such a way. Shouldn't he be called General Richardson? Instead of addressing him by his title and surname, he uses his first name, like children do in grade school. Is he missing something? In either case, he keeps his curiosity to himself as he observes the rest of the team.

Thom cuts off the officer with a wave of his hand and says, "Right, right, first, let's say hi to this very nice young man here. Everyone, I would like you all to meet Max. He is that shooter I have been talking about."

Everyone turns to appraise Max with testing eyes as they murmur to one another like clucking hens ready to peck on the unwelcome newcomer.

"A bit tiny, isn't he?" One of them smiles jokingly at Max, but his eyes show cool approval.

Max almost pouts, but he stops himself from doing so. He's always being called small and little by other people. Thankfully, he does not show his so-called puppy face to them. Thom smiles wanly and holds onto Max's shoulder with a comforting familiarity.

"Yep, he's my little puppy."

At that, Max has to scowl. Sure, he has been called that when he was younger, but they do not need to know that. Now that he is eighteen years old, he is a man and it is no longer appropriate. Instead, this term of endearment now sounds condescending and humiliating at the same time.

After all, a puppy blindly follows his master to the ends of the earth without a second thought. While he trusts his friend, he finds it highly inappropriate to address him as such in front of a group of strange men. As expected, the other officers laugh and smile at him, but there seems to be a little awkwardness among them.

Thom whispers to his friend, "You know I am just teasing," before leading him to a seat. Then, they begin to talk about a topic that is very popular among the Legion – the leader of the guerrillas, Trip. According to government records, Trip has never existed. He is said to be the cold-hearted killer full of hatred after he was shot three times in the chest. Somehow, he manages to survive, but no one knows how. Now, he runs the organization calls the Desiderios.

Max himself kind of admires their determination, but he will never admit that out loud. If he does, he will probably be hanged for being a traitor or be exiled without a second thought. The Legion is really against the idea that the guerrillas are any good at all.

Thom sighs and seats himself in one of the chairs. "Right, let's start with this meeting of ours."

The other officers look at Max with wariness. Thom looks next to him and sees Max looking very uncomfortable and smiles. "Don't worry. He's a unique case. I take full responsibility of him. So, he can listen in."

Usually, *privates* are not allowed to participate in these kinds of meetings with the high-ranking officers. They like to keep their strategies to themselves. There is no telling whether or not this lowly private is going to spill his gut to the others and jeopardize their plans.

Nevertheless, Thom is their superior. So, what he says goes. With slight hesitation, they all nod as one of them pulls out a notebook and starts to read off of it.

"There are recent reports of the Desiderios being spotted around the southern borders. There are still no sightings of their leader, but he is presumed to be hiding around the northern parts of the mountains around the south of the border where most of our sightings come from."

Thom interrupts him as he waves his hand at him. "That's just a guess. You never know. He can be up north or way west. That man moves everywhere quickly and never stays still for long. There are times when we spot him 100 miles away even though reports say that he is only 10 miles away. That's just how that man is."

They all frown at that, but no one dares to say anything. Thom yawns loudly and stands up.

"Come on, let's go, Max. I'll show you your quarters. I put you right beside me."

Max gets up alongside him, being completely overshadowed by his friend's shadow, and follows him out the door.

*

The remaining men in the room are infuriated by what they have just witnessed. First, they were late. Then, they leave after only a few minutes without having accomplished anything. The only thing they did was to meet his puny friend who does not deserve to be in the same room with them.

They wait until the boys are out of hearing range before they start talking again. The officers protest at the fact that they have all fought hard to earn their positions while that boy just waltzes in without any *real* experience. They are not going to lose their hard-earned positions to a little shrimp like him.

"The young man is too arrogant for his own good. He needs to be taken down a step." Lieutenant Gillnet makes the first comment.

"But he's protected by the commander. We can't do anything." Lieutenant Marcel says in frustration.

"Still, having a private attend a highly confidential meeting is ludicrous!" Major Fouke is obviously unhappy with the whole subject.

"Be patient. We'll figure it out soon. Right now, we just observe and follow to see where this all leads us. We don't want to arouse suspicions or cause any dissentions yet." General Hawk says as he tries to calm the others.

Even though he is the only one who also holds the rank of General, just like Thom, he has less authority. Unlike the others, however, he can wait. He can wait as long as he has to for what he deserved. Everyone understands what Hawk means as they all get up to go their separate ways. No one says a word afterwards.

*

Thom is walking alongside Max to the bunks when he stops suddenly at a fork in the hallways.

"By the way, I've decided to give you a full dorm to yourself. It's usually only for higher rank officers, but I gave you one right next to me. You're also going to be promoted to a field sergeant, like some of my subordinates."

At this, Max stops walking completely. "What! Why? I have to have many more years of service to have those positions."

"Oh, it's fine. I talked to the commander about it, and he says that as long as I trust you, you can be promoted as much and as quickly as I want." He chuckles at Max's wondering face and keeps walking.

"Come on." He calls out over his shoulder, "Don't be a slowpoke."

Max hurries up and walks beside him through the long corridors until they reach his room. It looks just like all of the other doors that they passed on the way there. He soon finds out why it is only for high ranking officers when the doors open to show a giant beautiful room.

It felt larger than his entire house itself. It had floor to ceiling windows on one wall, though they were covered with graceful curtains in a bright hue of blue.

The bed was a four-poster bed laden with pillows and sheets that he could just tell was silky and soft to the touch. A fireplace was situated across the room from the bed, and there was a thick rug placed right in front of it in the shape of a bear.

To his right was another door that led to who knows where as well.

It was perfect. It almost looked as though someone has made it specifically for him.

He turns and smiles at Thom before going to explore his new room. Thom grins as he watches him flit around like a little bird exploring its new surroundings.

When he finishes looking around, Thom leads him to the cafeteria to show him the other troops that he is going to be working with. They are mainly with the long-range sections as he is best with a gun. Initially, they all appear to welcome the young man to their ranks, but that all pretty much changed when Thom informs them that he is going to be their leader, not their comrade.

There are shouts of "What!" and "No way!" and the most common "He's just a child!"

"Sure, he is only 18, but he is perfectly capable of making his own decisions" is the answer that Thom gives.

After all, everyone else is at least a decade older than him, so he can understand their concerns. One of them makes sure that he lets Thom know that. To his disappointment, Thom just smiles and says, "Hey, he is the smartest in grade school. I bet he's still the smartest person in here now."

Max's mouth almost falls to the floor. That is his reasons for letting him become the boss of this group?! That's just a guess! He mentally smacks his head. That's Thom for you – smart but stupid at the same time.

The other men in the group have the same dumbfounded look on their faces and soon start to voice similar objections simultaneously.

People change.

Thom just shrugs them off with a smile. "See you later. Have fun." Max gawks at him as he leaves him with the other men.

Gregory, one of the privates amongst the group, sighs and puts his hand on his forehead. "That's him."

Max looks curiously at him. "What do you mean?"

"You don't know?" He shakes his head in disbelief. "Everyone knows that Thom is a very eccentric commander. He does the weirdest things sometimes."

"Yeah, he is always like that even when he is in grade school."

"So how was he like?" Gregory looks curious now.

"What do you mean?"

"As a child, you know. What was he like?"

Max laughs as he reminisces the old times, as if it was eons ago. "Oh you should have seen him. One time he…"

*

Thom smiles as he watches Max easily make friends with the rest of his group. Even when they were younger, he'd been able to get along with just about everyone. Of course, Max dragged Thom along as well. Unfortunately, Max was never interested in the Legion, so they never had that in common.

It looks to Thom that Max no longer wants to stay away from the Legion like he used to when he was younger. Hopefully, he doesn't, anyways. It would break his heart if he ever left the Legion without him.   Thom looks out toward the dismal lands that the headquarters overlooked. If he thought hard enough, he could just see the bloodied bodies left strewn around like dolls that would no longer see anything again. There were too many that he could see, far too many left dead in the Legion's wake.

It's too bad, really – just how messed up this land is.

*

Of course, being a childhood friend, Thom was not much older than Max, but they were quite different as well.

Unlike Max, he loves the Legion and excels at it. He rose through the ranks very quickly over the last five years, having won battle after battle as well as the hearts and admiration from the upper echelon. But, he is the exception. To think that his friend, who just joined the Legion, has already been promoted smells too much like favoritism – no matter how good he may be, which brings up the second, more important difference.

Thom is the son of the *real* leader of the Legion, General Victor Richardson – a fact that even Thom did not know for the longest time. During his childhood, he always thought that his father just worked a great deal, which explained why he was never at home much of the time. His mother often had a worried look on her face when he did not show up when she expected him, because that usually meant he'd been wounded and did not want to show up like that in front of his family.

Of course, she never showed her concerns to her son. Whenever he would be in the room, she would become cheerful again. She was so convincing that Thom never questioned her. When his father was home, he would shower him with gifts. Even though he knows it's no substitute for love, Thom was always very happy to receive them and treasured every moment he could spend with his father.

His mother never really told him what his father did for a living. All she would ever say is that he is a very important man and the country needs him, which always made him proud and that was all he needed to know. Believing that his father was a hero, Thom was always very confident with himself as he strived to be just like his old man.

Having been fighting for the Legion for the last 35 years, Victor has been wounded many times in battle and is quickly aging. Five years ago, he decided to bring his son and his childhood friend into the Legion, so he can prepare Thom to replace him and Max to support him. Before doing so, he made sure that no one knew that Thom was his son. By letting them go through the normal recruitment process, he hoped that the rest of his men would come to respect Thom and Max as their own men rather than because of his influence.

His plan was for Thom to be the face and Max to become the brain behind the operation. When Max decided not to join the Legion, Victor was a little surprised at first, but he never expressed it. He just discounted him as a pacifist who would prefer not to be involved in any form of violence. After all, he did not have the stature for physical prowess – and still doesn't.

Chapter 2: The Desiderios

"Trip! Trip! Where'd you go? We have to hurry!" Violet stomped up the corridor, searching for her leader.

She checked his room, his garden, and everywhere else she can think of until she finally gives up. Groaning, she sits down in disappointment. Of course, he picks now of all times to go and do his disappearing act on her. He's always been a little on the flighty side. Never staying in one place long enough before he moves onto the next one.

She's about to get up and try again when a hand clamps down on her shoulder. She lets out a shriek and turns around to face her childhood friend. "Do you always have to sneak up on me like that?!"

"Sorry." His voice, like always, is in a monotone voice. She sighs in relief.

"Well, now we can go, so let's hurry up! Let's go, go, go!" She pushes him down the hallway as she talks.

It is an odd sight. No matter how much she denies it, she is a super short young woman pushing and yelling at a tall, lean man with an emotionless face who looks like he can crush her at any second.

It's a regular thing to behold in the compound for the Desiderios guerillas, though. Violet is always pushing her best friend around, even though he is the leader and not her.

She steers Trip to the room that they are supposed to have been in 20 minutes ago and slams the door open.

"We're here!" The other people in the room look up from what they were studying and greet her and Trip.

"Hey! You guys finally made it!" Several of the members greeted them with grins on their faces. Unlike the government's Legion council, they all get along pretty well with the exception of one or two oddballs who consider themselves rivals.

"You shouldn't be so late to an important meeting." For example, Garrett is the glasses-wearing, studious, obsessive-compulsive man.

"It doesn't matter. We're not really doing anything." Then, we have Sunny, the lazy, easy-going kind of man. They hate each other's guts and will contradict and outdo one another no matter how trivial the conversation or task.

"You should understand the importance of being on time better, Sunny."

"And you should understand that nobody's perfect and on the dot all the time, ever. Not even you, so yeah." Sunny is little bit of a sarcastic person as well.

Garrett frowns and turns away as if he is saying, "You're not worth my time."

Violet smiles at their childish banter. It is always fun to see who will make the other one shut up faster. Usually, it's Sunny because he has better comebacks.

She steers Trip to his chair at the head of the table and plops down in her own one straight to the left of his. She claps her hands loudly and proclaims, "Alright! Fill us in. What are you men looking at?"

Garrett pulls out a folder and points to a picture. Violet squints at it and holds it close to her face. She can hardly tell what it is. It is too fuzzy. "What's this supposed to be?"

"This is a picture of the new recruit who has recently been inducted to the government's Legion. He was personally recommended by their acting commander, Thomas Richardson. His name is Max."

"Background, family, what about him?"

He shrugs his shoulders in response. "I couldn't find out what his family name is. It seems that he is a little bit of a mystery."

"Okay," Violet leans back into her seat. "Why does this child matter?"

"He was recently spotted at a guerilla hideout, mingling with the rest of the people. It also appears that he was promoted to a very high position in the Legion immediately after arriving."

While the Desiderios may promote those who are worthy earlier than expected, the Legion typically follow very strict rules for promotions. To deviate from the norm is highly unusual. And, anything out of the ordinary is cause for suspicion.

"There has to be a backstory to him – one that is much more interesting than him merely being the commander's friend. I am sure the commander has *many* friends. Is he one of us?" She was intrigued at the mention of his quick ascent through the ranks.

"That's the thing. We're not sure. He's obviously not harboring grudges against the guerillas considering how many times that he's visited the hangout these past few years."

"When did he start going over there? He may just be visiting a place that he used to go to before the war started six years ago."

"We thought about that, too, but he started visiting the area about one month *after* the war started, not before, which is a pretty good coincidence."

"That's not an uncommon thing, nowadays. He may just be a random child who is looking for a place to hide."

"He also spends a lot of time with Jordan talking about the Legion. From what he says, he seems to hate the Legion a whole lot."

"Why did he join them, then?" Violet asks the obvious question that is on everyone's mind.

"We don't know. That's why we are investigating him."

"Well, this is interesting. We have to quiz the child later on if we can catch him. What does he look like?"

"You can see him in the picture."

"I can't make out a thing from that fuzzy picture. For all I know, he looks like a bobcat."

Garrett sighs. "Alright, then, he's apparently pretty short, even for a child. And, he has brown hair and brown eyes – a regular appearance for a modern child these days. You probably will not even notice him unless you see him clearly."

"Well, that ought to narrow things down," Violet says sarcastically. "We need to keep an eye on him and find him later. Just see if we can have a talk with him. See if he's on our side or not."

"He's also a famous sharpshooter, under and aboveground. He's dangerous if he's not on our side."

Violet smiles. "Ah, now, that's a good reason for the Legion to want him. Well, that just means we better find him sooner than later."

She turns to look and see if Trip is willing to go along with it. Instead, she finds herself looking at an empty chair.

"Gaah! He's gone again!" She stands up and runs out the door mumbling, "He's always disappearing… that idiot…"

*

Trip was in his garden which is the only place that he's known to spend long periods of time in, tending to the small plants and flowers. The garden has always calmed him. Ever since he was on the brink of death, he's come to this place to enjoy the serenity.

This garden was the one that harbored all of his medicines that he needed during his recuperation. Violet and his garden are the only things that he treasures in this world.

On the other hand, there are times when Violet can get very annoying, but he can always count on the garden to be peaceful. So he often takes the time to escape here. That whole meeting was getting on his nerves the second that it started. Who cares about a child who appears to be on their side?

He never wanted to be here in the first place. The one and only reason that he is here is because of her. If he had a choice, he would be—

"Trip!" His thoughts are cut off when Violet barges into his garden. Trip mentally groans loudly in his head. She's back already! She points at him and starts to ramble on about the meeting. As always, he is not even listening when he suddenly interrupts her.

"Are those Asphodel?" Trip looks down to the flowers that he is tending.

Without realizing it, he was growing *those* flowers. For a second, it seems like the unthinkable has happened. Trip's face is twisted into one of regret and sorrow. It is only for a mere second. So fast that Violet wonders if she ever saw it in the first place.

"It's that day, huh?" She stares up at the cloudy sky. "I'll make sure no one disturbs you."

After that, she leaves him kneeling in the dirt, mourning as always, alone and silent.

*

Thom waltzes into Max's room without knocking to find that he is sound asleep on his bed. He smiles and strides over until he's next to him before leaning over and yelling in his ear, "Wake up!"

Max shoots up like a rocket and sits straight in bed yelling, "What?! What?!"

He's frantically trying to see who's there in the dark when he hears chortling from right in front of him, and he scowls.

Thom is laughing his head off by then. Max grimaces as soon as he catches sight of Thom and pushes him down.

"Man! What'd you do that for?"

"Ah, man, that was hilarious." Thom stops laughing after a little bit and suddenly looks at him seriously. "Oh, yeah, you're going on a mission."

"Okay, when is it?"

Thom grins at him and says, "In 30 minutes."

"Seriously?!" Max jumps out of bed and grabs his uniform and duffle bag as he hurriedly gets ready. "You should tell me this stuff at least a few hours beforehand."

He grabs his badge and starts fixing his hair in the mirror. "I need to get ready."

Thom waves his hand as he often does. "It's fine. It's just a small rendezvous to meet the corporal and his company. Afterwards, you are going to ambush the group of guerillas that are hiding out there. Except, *you* are going to be staying in the back, away from the rest of the hubbub."

"What?! Why?" He doesn't see why he has to stay away from the battle, especially if this is a mission. Thom smiles at him understandingly.

"You know that you are a long range fighter, so you have to stay away from the front line and go for the people from a distance."

Max groans with exasperation. He knows he's right and they both know that he knows. Thom gets up, puts his hands on his shoulders and says, "You'll get some of the action, too, so don't worry. Unlike all of the other recruits, you don't have to prove your worth. I know that you are the best that we can get."

Thom looks confident, but Max is not so sure. "Are you sure that I should be getting such special attention?"

Thom looks at him, surprised. "Of course! Why are you even asking? You are my best friend. How can you go wrong?" He smiles as he steers him towards the door, and they leave together with Max complaining about his hair.

*

Trip hides in the bushes with the rest of his crew. There are a dozen in all. Overall, they are a small group. They just found out that the Legion is planning to attack their campsite just over the hill.

Trip has Violet command all of them. She is basically the leader in all but name. He has attempted to give the title to her multiple times, but she has refused each and every time, insisting that he keep it.

She is happy enough giving out orders as second in command without having to have a *title* to weigh her down. Their spy comes back to them and relays the enemy's position to Violet and him. It's almost time. He is about to head to the front when she stops him by grabbing his shoulder. She seems to be a little excited.

"He's here." She does not have to specify anymore. The young man has been all she has talked about since she first heard about him. They only have a few sharpshooters, and apparently, he is the best of the best.

Trip nods in response and looks toward their campfire. A handful of the other men have started a fire and are sitting out in the open, tending to it. It is pretty obvious to the Desiderios that he is the bait. The rest of them are still hiding in the bushes. There is a rustling sound in front of them as a small squad tread down through the underbrush.

Violet signals to the rest of them, and they creep forward, silently. Half of them go around to the back and the other half head towards the front.

The Legionnaires rush in head on, the small squad believing they have the upper hand. The guerillas were ready, not nearly as relaxed as they made themselves off to be. The man that was leaning against the tree, supposedly on the watch but looking for all the world to be just lazing around, pulls out a semi-automatic in less than a breadth and starts picking off the Legionnaires.

Surprised, the front line fell quickly to the men in the camp, who were pulling out weapons one by one. Their captain shouted an order for them to retreat, but they barely started moving back when they were hit by the guerilla group in the rear.

The captain receives a blade to the back before he could change their direction once more, and the remainder of the squad was left on the defensive.

It seems like the guerillas are winning when suddenly, one of their commanding officers falls to the ground before he can even utter a sound. Trip narrows his eyes. That was an expert shot, only hitting the shoulder, enough to incapacitate but not to kill. It seems there's a skilled shooter on the enemy's side, and, judging by Violet's excited face, it's the boy.

She gives him a grin before slipping down into the thick of the fighting, her blades flashing and gun fire surrounding her figure as men fell to the ground all around her. Owning up to her nickname "The Warrior".

He sighs and shakes his head before a glint catches his eye. He peers closer, moving silently through the underbrush. That looked suspiciously like the scope of a gun.

He skirts the edges of the battle, keeping an eye at all times on the glint. When he's half way there, a shot rings out, and a guerilla man falls to the ground. Trip grimaces and moves faster. He was downing all of their men.

He slips around a tree to see a small clearing that overlooks the raging battle. A young man was crouching behind a bush with his gun to his eye. Trip starts heading up to where he is when he hears a crack.

He stops and is as still as possible for a moment when he hears a gentle crackling sound. It's the trees moving with the body attempting to be silent. They are not very quiet. Trip waits until the person is close enough to touch before shooting a poison dart into his chest. He covers the man's mouth with his hand before gently laying the body to the ground. He loathes the idea of using loud weapons like guns to fight. There is too much mess to clean up after and he is not a fan of all of the blood spilled.

The young man aims straight at Violet. Trip is right behind him. As he cocks the gun, Trip puts his hand on the young man's shoulder gently. Shocked by the unexpected intruder, the young man almost drops his gun in fear.

"Ahhh!" He twists around, and if it is possible, looks even more frightened as his face turns as pale as a sheet.

Anybody would be terrified to see a man dressed in all black wearing a ski mask staring them in the face. He tries to get away from him as much as he can by leaning deeper into the bushes, but his struggle is useless.

"W-who a-are you?" His voice comes out shakily.

Trip stares into his eyes through his mask. He is a rookie – a very scared one at that. "You will know." He utters a single sentence before a tranquilizer dart is put in his neck.

This one is not enough to kill him but is just enough to knock him unconscious for a few hours.

Trip grabs his gun in one hand and his body in another as he heaves them both over his shoulder. He uses his fingers to whistle a distinct sound. Hearing the signal, his men fall back and run into the shadows.

The rest of the sharpshooter's group is left looking at them with bewilderment, but none of them run after the guerillas. Trip runs through the forest to the trucks that are waiting for them. Violet and the rest of the men are already inside, signaling them to hurry up. She makes sure that all of the wounded have been rescued and are receiving immediate medical assistance, including the ones that were shot by this young man.

Trip drops his body into the seat next to him but keeps a firm grip on the gun. He motions for some of the men to tie him up. They don't know for sure which side he is on yet. Violet sits next to him and studies the young man.

"Isn't Max so innocent looking?" She smiles at the small man who is tied up like a hog. "It would be great if he ends up on our side, but don't you find it odd?'

Trip looks at her with a blank stare. Violet takes that to mean that he thinks it is odd as well. He never answers her questions, so she starts to guess by looking at the smallest changes of his expression – not that there is much to work with, especially with a ski mask on.

"He never killed anyone. All of the shots that came from his position were meant to wound, not kill. He might just be on our side."

Trip nods, and they settle down for the rest of the ride while the young man lies in the back of the van in silence.

*

Max awakens to find himself in a dark room. He's lying on a bed, one that was much smaller than his own at the Legion headquarters, but almost as comfy.

He reaches out in front of him, but he can't even see his hands. This wasn't good. Was he captured? He couldn't tell, and he was starting to panic.

He sits up quickly, but that just makes it worse. His breath comes in short gasps, and his eyesight is spotty. He is almost hyperventilating when the door slams open in front of him, letting in just enough light to see a silhouette, but nothing more.

Trying to get a better sense of his surroundings, he lies completely still and doesn't move an inch from his spot on the bed. A few seconds go by before the person starts talking.

"I know that you're awake." It is a small, young woman. She keeps on talking when he just stares and says nothing.

"We have cameras. I didn't want you to be cramped up in this little room, but Trip says that he doesn't trust you. Well, he doesn't *say* that, exactly, but I get the point. He's a big party pooper, but he is my best friend, so you know, you like to go along with your best friend."

At the words *best friends*, Max relaxes a little. He is pretty sure that if a person is able to be nice to a close friend, he probably is not all that bad of a person and, perhaps will not treat him too badly.

He gets a better look at the young woman. He is surprised to find that she is so little. He cannot see her face since she is still in the shadows, but he doesn't say anything. The young woman seems to be able to tell what he is going to say, and she flips on the switch. Instantly, light floods the room.

He shields his eyes and squints as he looks up at her. Now that he can see, he notices that she is smiling brightly at him. It is like she is excited to be able to see him for the first time.

"It's so great to see you Max!" Violet shouts.

Max looks at her curiously. It seems that she knows him somehow. They must have either been planning this, or they found his name in the records.

"We found you when you enrolled in the government's Legion. Don't worry about the treatment. This is standard procedure for the rookies that we get from the Legion."

"How did she—?" It's like she can read his mind.

The young woman giggles at him. "Oh, don't worry, I am not psychic. I'm just really good at reading people's expressions. It's very useful when Trip decides to stop talking, which he does, a lot."

Max watches curiously as she sits down on the bed next to him. She is opening up a lot to a total stranger. He wonders if she is always like this with other people.

"Oh, and…"

She cuts off what she was saying when a figure walks by the open doorway.

"Trip! Trip! Come over here!" It's the same person who took him by surprise on the battlefield. He's not wearing the face mask anymore, but Max can tell that it's the same man just by the way he carries himself so confidently and so calmly and the black, of course.

His hair is lazily pulled up in a ponytail, and he's wearing a plain black t-shirt with a black military-style jacket. His heavy-looking boots, fingerless gloves, and black jeans complete the look. The entire ensemble gave him the creepy vibe.

He's this bright lady's best friend? She looks the exact opposite with a purple shirt and short jean shorts. It looks like she is ready for the beach, and he is ready for a blizzard.

The young woman puts her hand on Max's shoulder and smiles comfortingly at him. "This morbid man is my best friend. He's called Trip, but I think that your government rats call him El Diablo or something stupid like that."

El Diablo, the devil, is the name that Trip was nicknamed after his little stint with the three bullets in his chest. To the rebels, it is a term of admiration to show he is almost superhuman. Of course, the Legion may not interpret it that way.

Max's mouth almost falls to the ground. This is the infamous El Diablo! How can it be? No one has ever seen him since the incident!

Yet, here he is, looking like he has never been hurt in his life. Not only is there no wobble or limp in his walk, he does not look like he is even having any trouble breathing considering that the shots were straight in the chest. What is he made out of? Steel?

"W-wait! Doesn't that mean that since you're his best friend that you're..." The young woman smiles cheerfully at him.

"Yep! I'm the Warrior. You can call me Violet, though."

Max leans forward and massages his temples. "This is too much to process right now."

"What do you mean?" Her voice is right next to him. He looks up to see her gazing at him from underneath.

"Ah!" He jumps up and moves away from her. She pouts at him when he scoots away. Anybody in their right mind would be scared of being in the same room as El Diablo and the Warrior.

He voices his thoughts aloud, and her smile falls.

"Well, that's mean! Trip and I are perfectly fine. We're no different from either you or the rest of the citizens. We are, however, very different from those government rats. Right, Trip?"

They both turn to look at an empty doorway.

"Gaah! He's gone…again! Ugh, I will catch up with him later. In the meantime, now that you know who we are, why don't you start by telling us a little more about yourself?" Violet says as she crosses her arms.

"Well, my name is Max, but you already know that."

"Max what? Just Max?"

"Sullivan. Max Sullivan."

After her intelligence team failed to come up with his family name, Violet has been eagerly anticipating the answer. Now that she hears it, she finally understands why the Legion wants him.

Not to give away her thoughts, she extends her hand and says, "Welcome, Max Sullivan, it's very nice to be formally introduced to you. Is there anything else you want to tell me about yourself?"

"What would you like to know?"

"Anything you would like to share is okay with me. I'm not picky."

"Mmmm. I am 18 years old and I am an only child."

"Congratulations! You are now a man, sort of," Violet says teasingly.

"My best friend's name is Thom. We've been buds since we were five."

"That's really sweet! It's kind of like me and Trip!"

Max couldn't really think of anything else that stood out in his life. Violet notices this and stands up.

"Well, now that the ice is broken. I trust that we can be friends soon enough. Now, I have to go. See ya!"

She races out of the door and is about to close it shut when she sticks her head through the opening.

"I'll come see you tomorrow." She winks at him before closing and locking the door. Max sighs and flops back down on the bed. He has to think about all of this. This is just so confusing.

*

Violet trots down the corridors. Where is Trip? She already looked in the garden, but he wasn't there. She has to find out where he is. He probably didn't even care to listen to anything that she told him. That is just like Trip to forget everything that's important.

After a few minutes of roaming around, she goes to his room and knocks on the door, hoping that he is there. He is often in his room during the early morning hours. Trip knows that she is the only one who even dares to knock. Violet is glad to hear that he is in when a series of sounds ring out when he unlocks each and every one of his dozen door locks. Trip takes his privacy very seriously.

The door swings open to reveal a pitch-black room. A small sliver of light is intruding the room through a crack in his curtains. He always has the oddest habits of keeping his room in precise order. And he thinks Garret has a problem.

Violet steps through and sits delicately in one of his lounge chairs. He will not tolerate any loud ruckus near him. Trip is lying on the bed, quietly and motionlessly.

"Why'd you go?" Her voice is soft and quiet in the silent room.

"Does it matter?" He speaks in his monotone voice that he's adapted to using all the time. Whenever Violet is in his room is the worst time. She finds it even harder to tell what he genuinely thinks about because it is difficult to tell from just his voice when they are in complete darkness.

"Yeah, it kind of does. He can be a very valuable person to us if you'd just reach out to him."

"You will do fine."

Violet sighs. "Just because I can do it myself doesn't mean that I will always be able to do it alone. You're my best friend, and you're the reason that I'm still alive. But I also need you even when my life is *not* in danger, okay?"

Trip does not respond.

She gets up and leaves the room as quietly as she can.

*

The truth of the matter is, Violet saved Trip as much as he saved her. Trip hadn't always been a doom and gloom type of man and didn't always wear all black. When he was a child, his life was quite blissful. In fact, he was very outgoing and loved nature. Even though he didn't have much growing up, he loved every minute of it. Where he's from, flowers were not as pretty as the ones he's been tending in the garden today, but nonetheless were still very beautiful.

He comes from a land called Algoma, commonly known as the Land of the Desert, a neighboring town outside of Balavan where the Legion presides.

Despite its arid terrains, his hometown was filled with colorful blossoms like the desert willow, blue phacelia, golden snapdragons, and silky dalea. Even the prickly cantus flowers bloom beautifully.

He enjoyed lying next to these flowers at night when there was a cool breeze. He always looked forward to the tranquility of the night skies and thought life could not be more perfect.

His people were a quiet and hardworking group. They always minded their own business and no one really cared to bother them because they live on what looks like a wasteland to outsiders. With a lot of sweat and painstaking work, they were able to turn the desert into farmlands. They were content tending their cattle and sheep as well as nurturing their corn fields.

All that changed when the Legion decided to invade it many years ago. One day, a troubling rumor started to spread that eventually led to Algoma's demise. Word spread that there was a large amount of oil just waiting to be harvested underneath their world of sand. No one knew where the rumor came from, but the damage was already done.

Within weeks, the Legion's men came in the thousands. Trip's parents, along with other brave men and women fought gallantly against the invaders, while the children hid. But, alas, they were no match for the well-disciplined Legion of the west. Because it'd been a long period of peaceful silence, they did not have the training nor proper weapons to defend their land. Within days, Algoma was burned to the ground and both of his parents were dead and so were most people he knew.

Eager to get what they came for, the Legion paid little attention to the children who were crying or wandering the streets. The ones that annoyed them or attempted to attack them were immediately killed off.

Most hid, still waiting for their mothers and fathers to come back to them.

They ransacked and plundered everything, taking anything of value. They even took the clothes off of the corpses along with their jewelries and shoes, leaving the mangled dead bodies lying in the middle of the road in disarray.

Then, they brought in large drills, backhoes, and excavators to dig around the entire land haphazardly for what they expected to be the mother lode – the natural resources that started the whole escapade. Before long, they realized that there was no oil, no gemstones, and no previous gold to be found anywhere on this barren land. It was nothing more than dirt and sand.

In the midst of the pillaging frenzy, Trip noticed a man on the horseback who stood out from all of the others as he hid behind rubble. Very few people ride horses these days, except for those who are nostalgic of the prim and proper days.

He had piercing blue eyes and a large scar over his left cheek. From his closely buzzed hair and clean shaven face to his starched stiff uniform and shiny boots that were now stained with the blood of his victims, it was obvious, even to a mere child, that this was the commander who led the devastating war against his people.

From his facial expression, it was also pretty clear that he was frustrated with the results, but nevertheless, he let his men do as they pleased. After a day of fighting, his men always want to blow off steam. If they don't do it on the battlefield, they often do it in a bar or on the streets later, causing him more headaches. After they were satisfied with their loot, the Legion soon left almost as quickly as they came – leaving behind nothing but a literal waste land of death and destruction.

At the tender age of seven, Trip was an orphan. He had no home to go to and no one to turn to. He could not understand why these people came to his home and killed everyone. They've never done anything to anyone to deserve this. All he knew was he had to survive to avenge his parents. He dried his tears away and strived to live once more.

For the next few weeks, he wandered along the desert road by himself, not knowing where to go or whether or not he will live to see the next day. His canteen was already empty and he hadn't had a meal in days. He survived on whatever berries and occasional edible bugs he could pick off of the land, which was not much. He was so weak that he could no longer feel anything, not the hunger, not the thirst, and not his toes. He had no idea that his feet were bleeding and his throat was so dry that he could no longer utter a sound.

When he thought for sure that he was going to die, a caravan arrived. He thought it was a mirage and instantly collapsed. But, it was not a dream or an illusion.

It was the Kerbasians, a nomad tribe that passed through that area once a year. They had been known to trade with the Algomians and were on their way to conduct their usual business when they witnessed the devastation that the Legion left behind.

As they passed by the desert land, Trip's homeland was still smoldering. When they came upon the poor boy, they picked him up and nursed him back to health. Days, then weeks, went by before he awoke from his deliria. The first person he saw was Violet, a mere child of only five years old, leaning over him with a worried expression far too old for her age.

She'd been by his side tirelessly since they picked him up from the desert, wiping his head with cold towels to keep down his fever and comforting him in his restless sleep. When he regained his consciousness, she was glad that he was finally back to almost normal health.

Even though she was too young to understand what happened to Trip, she knew that he was all alone and needed someone. She was happy to be the one who was there for him. The first thing he heard was her cheerful voice saying "Hi, stranger! Glad to see you are awake! My name is Violet. Nice to meet you!"

At the sound of her friendly voice, he cracked a weak smile. He knew that he was safe and in a peaceful place the second he heard her.

He never forgot that moment and was very grateful to her and her family for saving him from certain death. From that moment on, they were best of friends, watching out for each other's backs.

At the same time, he never forgot the face of the man on the horse who led the destruction of his home and the murder of his parents. Over the next few years, he traveled with Violet's people and became stronger with each passing day. As they traveled, he learned about other people and started to understand how the world works.

He understood how the world was cynical and dangerous, that in order for him to survive, he had to be strong, much stronger.

He grew up with Violet, telling her his past and history, yet leaving out the details from the siege that were too graphic for an innocent girl to hear.

Their connection was stronger than anything, forging a bond that would never be broken over time.

She became his partner in his journey for revenge against the Legion. Together, they earned names of fear, and legends were made of them.

And, when the time came, they were ready for war.

Chapter 3: Max's Journal

Thom couldn't believe it. Max was gone. He rushed to Max's room. Where was he? It's been 24 hours since the mission ended with the guerillas oddly backing out, and no one has seen hide or tail of him. The rest of the men under his command already tried searching for him when he didn't show up after the head count.

He couldn't figure out just where he'd gone. He couldn't have left the Legion. Could he? He knows that Max has always hated the government, but he had hoped that his views changed enough for him to enroll. Is it possible that he went AWOL? No.

He shakes his head back and forth. He has to trust him and hope that he will show up soon. Thom opens the door to his room. Perhaps, he has left some clues as to what may have happened to him. He looks through his desk and is pawing through the papers that Max had left, which was an amazing amount for someone who just arrived, when his hand hits something.

"Hmm?" He pulls out a book from the recesses of the drawer. It was small and black, so it blended in with the drawer. It wasn't particularly well hidden, but he was only here for a few days. It was probably the best that he could do.

He opens the book and flips through the first page. It's a journal. He grows excited at the possibilities of what is written inside. The first page is dated May 4, 2086. That was the day that the Legion first approached him about the prospects of joining them. He sits down on Max's bed and reads through the rest of the page.

*

May 4, 2086

Today, I saw Thom talking to this big, bulky guy with no hair. He seemed kind of intimidating, but I later saw him addressing the rest of the school about a meeting. This guy was from the army. I don't like the army. Stupid, useless, fighting machines that will accomplish nothing with their pointless killing that they are doing.

When Thom saw my face when he started talking about joining the Legion, he started looking at me all weird like. It took me a little bit to realize that I had a horrible look on my face.

That is my mistake. I know that I shouldn't have shown him my "bad" face. He is too innocent to see my dreadful side. I wish that he would not go and join the Legion. I know that he won't if I ask him not to, but I will let him make his own decisions. If he joins, I will know what he chooses.

*

Thom smiles at Max's words, "Too innocent? He thinks *I* am too innocent?" All this time, Thom thought he was the one protecting his friend, but now he sees that the feeling is quite mutual. He hopes his friend is tough enough to handle whatever situation he's in right now. No matter what is going on, he hopes that he is safe out there as he continues to read the next entry.

*

May 25, 2086

Today, I overheard some of the teachers talking. They are saying that we are too young to know about the war. It's too bad that they don't know that some of the children dream about being in the war and being heroes for their countries.

I try hard not to laugh hysterically in their faces when they start going off. Thom did it, too. I think that he is thinking seriously about whether to join or not. He kept asking me about it, but I refuse to mess with his choice. I can't influence what he chooses to do.

Today, the big, bald man came to our school again. He is the Legion freak that I don't like. He took some of the more athletic children who were in our gym class and set them aside to talk to them.

Thom is with them. Later, he started spouting on about how great it is to be in the Legion. I did not say anything, but I think he can tell that I was not happy.

*

Thom stops there for a second. He remembers when that whole thing happened. After that, he sensed that they were a little distant from each other. He used to wonder about it, but now he knows.

*

November 21, 2086

I haven't seen Thom all summer. I've been in my parents' estate, out here in the country, where the war has not ravaged the land and its people. I don't think he knows where I am. When I finally saw him again, he was a little angry at me. It's probably because I never contacted him like I promised to, but I cannot. Outside phone calls are not allowed where I am. I left this journal in my apartment, so I couldn't go back to get it. If Thom knows what is happening, he will hate me anyways, so I let him have his petty anger for a little while.

When he told me that he tried to call my parents, I have to grit my teeth to stop from shouting everything I know. I haven't really told him anything about my parents for the last few years. He knew them when we were younger, but after that, I stopped talking about them. I don't think that he noticed.

He still doesn't even think about the times when I left for weeks on end to 'visit my parents'. Either he's really oblivious, or he's just deciding to not pry into my business. I guess that's one reason why we are best friends. Neither one of us wants to get into one another's business without being invited to — no matter how much we want to.

In any case, I hope that he never finds out, or, at least, he will never ask.

*

Well, Max definitely got one thing right. Neither one of them wanted to influence the other, until now anyways. But then again, a part of him wishes that they *would* try to tell the other what he is thinking. That way, they can avoid all of this guessing and worrying. They *are* still best friends; after all, at least Thom hopes they are.

*

December 2, 2086

I haven't attended school for a long time. I've been working in the backgrounds where my parents left off. I think that Thom is just waiting for the chance to leave and go to boot camp. It starts in January, and he already told me that he's leaving. I didn't show any signs of sadness, so I think that he was a bit disappointed with me. Maybe he was hoping that I would change my mind and join him or beg him not to go, but I was not about to do either.

It is impossible for me to show any sign of happiness for a man who is going to join the Government and be their killing machine, so I left and went to work for my parents.

*

Thom closes the book with a snap when he is jolted by a knock on the door.

"Pardon me, Sir! Can you come with us immediately? There is a meeting that you must attend to!"

It seems that they knew that he would be in Max's room.

"Let them know that I will not be attending anything for the next few days!"

There is a short pause before he yells out, "Yes, Sir!"

Thom sighs and falls back on his bed. Now that he remembers, he did wonder about Max's parents. He's apparently "working" for them. He hasn't seen Max's parents in years. They probably don't even know that Thom's in the Legion now, let alone the general.

He sighs and lies back down. He would figure it out in the morning. He closes his eyes and falls into an uncomfortable slumber.

*

Thom wakes with a start when his hand hits something hard. He looks around his surroundings. Where is he? This isn't his room. What is he doing here – still in full military uniform? Then he looks at what his hand hit, and he remembers. He is in Max's room, and he's been reading his journal from a few years ago. He opens the blinds and turns the page to where he left off.

*

December 25, 2086

I am all alone on this dreadful holiday. I woke up this morning with a sense of total and utter emptiness. Right now, I am back in my parent's old estate. This Christmas will not be a jolly one for me as I am pretty much alone with no one I love to celebrate this holiday with.

Thom left to go and visit his family about a week ago. I also left that same day, but it is not to visit my family. It is to go to a rendezvous at the hideout. These are some dangerous, unhappy holidays for me. So far, my holiday has consisted of making a few dozen bombs, fixing up my parents' old laboratory and tending the old rose garden. I will have to go and tend to the family graves later on. The flowers there are wilting.

Thom just called me. He is excited over some trivial thing that is insignificant to me. I pretended that I am thrilled for him, though. I made sure to hang up with some excuse before he can ask me about my Christmas. I wonder if he bought it, or he is just that dense. I'm sure that he is just dense.

I must go. The doorbell has rung. I know that it is the people from the hideout. If they find out that I am writing in a journal, they will surely take it away from me. Then they will find out about Thom, and I cannot let that happen.

*

Thom snaps the book closed with a sigh. He's been protecting him. From what, though? What is so bad that he has to secretly record his thoughts into a journal that he can never let anyone see? What is that sentence about making bombs about as well? He really hopes that Max hadn't been involved in a scandal when they were younger.

When they were thirteen, Max was a model student who aced all of his tests, so he was never a troublemaker, but it seems that he's involved with some heavily secret organizations.

Thom thinks about the time that they were separate during that Christmas. Like Max wrote, he hadn't even thought about what Max sounded like. He'd been too happy about getting what he wanted for Christmas.

He sighs. Maybe he has been too insensitive about Max's problems. He never listened to him, but he never asked to tell him anything, either! He never talked about his personal problems. He always brushed it off whenever something happened to him. That is just the way he is. They never get all sentimental about anything with one another.

Perhaps, the next entry will show some insight into his complex mind.

*

January 9, 2087

Today, they came. I don't know what happened, but one of them got mad at me because he accused me of making the wrong thing for him. I tried to tell him that he just picked up the wrong one, but he would not listen. The man beat me up for no reason at all!

Now I'm stuck with a messed up face and broken bones. I have to go to a hospital and get it all splinted up. When the doctor asked what happened to me, I told him that I fell down the stairs. I'm pretty sure that he did not believe me at all. When he asked me again, I told him that I was going to be fine as soon as he fixed me up, and he left it after that. I obviously was not going to tell any of them what happened.

*

Again, who are *they*? Are they the people from the hideout? Are they members of the guerrillas? He does not know. Max is not even fully truthful to himself in this journal, let alone truthful to anyone else. Even though Max seems to be divulging so much in these journals, it's hard to tell exactly what he is divulging. Is he trying to warn others? Or, is he trying to call for help? The cryptic writing only makes it so much more frustrating.

Thom sighs. What is he going to do with Max? If he is indeed a part of the guerrillas, that would be a problem, for both of them. After all, he was the one who dragged Max into the Legion. That is as good as vouching for him. If Max is with the enemy, what now? He has to protect his friend, but first he has to understand him.

It's been 3 days since he vanished without a trace, and he is no closer to finding out what has happened to him. The next one is a long entry.

*

I no longer attend school. It's a hard adjustment for me, but I'll work it out. Thom has been in boot camp for the last month, but we maintain a steady friendship. I held a gun for the first time since my parents'... disappearance. I can now say it in this journal without feeling remorse even though I still cannot say it out loud.

Crow is my shooting teacher. He forged my path to becoming a sharpshooter. I now do competitions and fight with other trainees. It helps that I have natural talent, but I fear that the others do not feel so pleased with me. I've heard them talking. There is a conspiracy under foot. I know that I will be in danger if I confront them, so I left the training sessions but make sure that I keep my gun handy.

Crow has found me multiple times, asking why I was not there. I don't answer him. He must not be able to tell. Even when I'm not there, the other trainees hate me. Ever since my recruitment, the expectations have grown higher because of me. They blame their failure to please their officers on me. I don't bother to correct them. There is no point. They are angry, simple as that. I can do nothing about it. I will just bear it for now.

Now that I am no longer part of the shooting sector, I work in the Mech section working on rebuilding engines for all sorts of things. Even though it's very different from shooting, I got the hang of it pretty quickly. I guess I am just good with my hands. It takes my mind off of other things — things that I would rather not think about. All that does is get my spirits down and I cannot let that happen.

I need to keep up my appearances, which is much easier to do here underground. I love it here. It is good work, and nobody loathes me. I can now stay out of the way. Another good thing is that my name is no longer known. People here like to use nicknames. They just call me Newbie. Nobody really cares what other people call one another either. Like, there is the Big Guy, the Genius, and the Man. It is easier to hide this way. I don't want to be a public figure. And, apparently, neither does anyone else in this joint. Sometimes I wonder what everyone else has to hide, but, then again, others may be wondering the same about me.

It has been a long time since I've seen the civilians. I've been concealed in the underground, working. It takes a long time to do what I do. Today, I overheard them talking, and I realized that this whole thing is led by a few people.

Names are thrown around, but only a few are constant. El Diablo is what they are calling him now. Nobody has mentioned what his name used to be or dared to find out anything else about him because they are too scared to get close to him. It is a fitting nickname for him, though. After all, who else will ever be able to survive three bullets to the chest besides the Devil himself?

Another is Violet: the roughest, meanest warrior there. Rumor has it she can take out an entire Legion squad before anyone even sees her coming. If they do get a glimpse of her on the battlefield, it would be the last thing they will ever see. I have also heard that she enjoys an occasional glass of her enemy's blood for breakfast, but I am not so sure if I believe that. Some of the other men sure look like they do.

There are at least fifteen other names that are talked about. Each one sounds terrifying, but those two stand out the most. They say that you should fear for your life if you ever come in contact with them. At least, that's what I hear. I don't know what to believe, but I have to do it. I have to do it for my parents. Wonder what does the Legion really think of them?

*

Thom sighs and shuts the book. Now he knows what Max was doing during those years. He had attempted to find out where he moved to, but no one knew. That's because he didn't move. He'd been working with the Desiderios. Perhaps that is what he is doing now. He groans in frustration and puts his head in his hands. Why is Max doing this? It all has to be connected somehow. Something must be encouraging Max to do this, but what?

After reading Max's journals, Thom has to gather his thoughts and decide what to do. It took him a long time and a great deal of effort to bring Max *into* the Legion, but to what end? He had to convince the people in the Legion headquarters that, despite his small physique and his lack of desire to join the Legion when the recruiters first approached him, Max is an asset that the Legion needs.

When he found out that Max was a sharpshooting champion, he was overjoyed because he finally had a slam dunk reason to bring him in. The Legion can always use a good sharpshooter. He never once bothered to ask himself how in the world a little bookworm like Max became such a good shot so quickly in the first place. He just assumed that he had a natural gift, and never bothered to ask him. Now, he wonders if Max would have told him about this mysterious Crow person that he wrote about in his journal.

After finally getting the OK, Thom also spent numerous hours trying to locate him. It was by chance that he bumped into Max that day on the streets when he dragged him to the Legion headquarters with him. That day, Thom was so happy. He thought he did his childhood friend a big favor. After all, everyone who is in the Legion lives comfortably and seems to be quite happy, at least compared to everyone else in the dominion.

Now, he is sorely disappointed to know that that is not the case. All of his efforts were a waste. He's kicking himself for not seeing any of the signs before making a fool of himself parading his friend around like he was a war hero or something in front of the high ranking officers who were already jealous of *him*.

Back then, he thought the only reason for Max's resistance was because of his pacifist view. His friendship completely blinded him to any other possibility. Never once did he ever imagine that his friend may have already committed himself to another military group, especially not one that is *against* his own.

In hindsight, he did see some red flags. Even though he went to his parents' home many times to find Max, he was usually not there. There were times when he thought that Max was indeed home, but pretended not to be so he didn't have to open the door. At the time, Thom was a little upset just thinking of the possibility.

When he did open the door, Max was always very quiet about what he was doing. Of course, it was Thom's fault for not asking, but, once again, he wonders what Max would have said if he asked.

Now that he knows what Max is doing, he cannot let him get back into the Legion. The other officers will definitely accuse him of treason and try to kill both of them. They have always wanted an excuse to dispose of him to begin with. He cannot let that happen. He has to hide these journals so no one can find them before he finds the truth from his friend personally.

No matter what, he knows Max is a good man and he has to have a good reason for joining the Desiderios. Even though he fears the worst, he is not going to jump to any conclusions. He is determined to give him the benefit of the doubt and protect him like he knows his friend would do for him if their positions were reversed.

Maybe he was being blackmailed.

The thought comforts him. After all, there is no way his friend would willingly go against him, is there? But, then again, what possible reason can someone have to blackmail him?

The only way to find out is to find him. But, where? The Desiderios is very good at covering their tracks. The

Legion has been searching for their hideout for many years, but no one has ever found them or at least come back alive to report it. Putting the journal snugly in his inside pocket, he goes in search of his friend.

Chapter 4: The Training

Max wakes up in an unfamiliar place. It's small and comfortable, but it isn't a place he remembers. He sits up and changes into another pair of clothes before walking around and freshening up.

He walks up to his door and does a cursory check of attempting to open the door. He's not expecting it to even open, but to his surprise, it does.

He steps out into the hallway and looks around before realizing that no one is standing guard over him.

He is wandering around the rebel headquarters when he reaches a door that's ajar. Being a curious person, he goes and knocks on the door. The door opens a second later, and to his surprise, Violet's head pops out.

She gives him a large grin and steps out of the room. "Hey, Max!"

Max gives a little smile in response.

"How do you like this place?"

"It's nice."

"Uh huh, I'm sure it's different from what you're used to. Why don't you go outside? It's a beautiful place right now."

"Sure, uhmm… exactly how do I get out, by the way?"

Violet smiles and gives him some directions to the side door that leads outside.

Unfortunately, the building is far too large, and he gets lost trying to find the door. After wandering about for a little bit, he spots a door that leads outside and decides that he will take his chances and see if there is a mine field out there or a meadow filled with flowers.

To his surprise, and happiness, he finds that he is entering a well-kept garden. There are rows of herbs, flowers, and vegetables that are neatly organized. A garden arbor with a bench underneath is set in the corner of the garden. A high stone wall serves as the border around the garden. A walkway leads to an area with trees for shade and a picnic table set. A hammock is strung between two trees, and there appears to be a person lying in it.

Max looks closer and sees that it is Trip. He has his eyes closed, so he is probably asleep, or at least pretending to be.

He slowly starts to back up and accidentally trips over one of the borders. Not wanting to awaken Trip, he grits his teeth to hiss quietly in pain and wipes his hands off. When he gets up, Max looks up and finds Trip standing up, watching him.

"Ah!" Max almost jumps a foot in the air. He was sure that he was asleep just seconds ago. And he was trying to be invisible, too. Obviously, his attempt at exiting quietly failed miserably.

He manages to sum up the courage to ask him something else he is curious about. "Why are you here?"

Trip stares at him before saying, "It's my garden."

"Oh," Max chuckles nervously. "Well, I am, you know, just walking by, and I accidentally walked past this place. Sorry, you know, if I am intruding or anything." He's backing up slowly the whole time he's talking, and Trip notices it.

He steps forward and grabs his arm, stopping his retreat. Max smiles feebly. What is he going to do to him? He is not mad, is he? His thoughts are tumbling, but it ends up being unnecessary. A mere five minutes later, he is weeding out the garden while Trip is watering them.

To his complete surprise, he is the one who planted all of these flowers. He figured that Violet, the happy and jolly woman who loves colors, would naturally be the one who designed and cultivated the plants while Trip merely wanders around the grounds as a sanctuary. But he was wrong.

Apparently, Trip spends more time here than anywhere else. He is the one who decides which flower complements which shrub to give it the right ambiance. The garden is also filled with such delicate fragrance. Every area seems to have a different theme. One section is sweet and elegant while another is fresh and peaceful.

He makes Max go and start weeding the rest of the vegetables. He quickly complies and starts working. After those few words, Trip doesn't say anything else to him except to tell him to go and help weed out the rest of the plants.

He's almost done when Violet comes bouncing up to the gate and starts pounding on it.

"Trip! Where are you? It's time for dinner."

Max gets up, and Violet looks at him in surprise. "Max! I didn't know you were here. How do you like it?"

She is about to say more when Trip appears next to her suddenly, and she shrieks.

"Oh my gosh! Trip, stop doing that!" Her hand is over her heart as she stares at Trip. He just gazes at her with a blank face. She turns back to Max and smiles.

"You'll love dinner. It's when all of the higher-ups gather together, and we argue like a big family. It's fun! We make all of the food from the gardens, too!"

She opens the gate and grabs Max's hand, "But first, we have to get you two all cleaned up."

She turns around and pats Trip on the shoulder before grabbing Max and pushing them into the building. Max is then herded to his room and forced to take yet another shower before Violet dresses him up in some fashionable clothes fit for a classy dinner.

They meet up with Trip in the hallway, and Violet starts rebuking him for not dressing within her 'dress code'. He's wearing the exact same thing that he was wearing earlier except for the fact that all of the dirt is gone from gardening. He probably has multiple copies of the same outfit.

Violet sighs in disappointment and stops in front of a door. She flings it open with a dramatic push. "People, we have arrived! Let the feast commence!"

In front of them is a table with seats filled with people who range from prim and proper to loud and obnoxious. It seems that Violet has made sure they all wore something presentable. They, however, each undid something in order to make themselves more comfortable.

Violet drags Max around the table with a smile and starts introducing him to everyone.

"This is Sunny." Sunny smiles at Violet and gives Max a lazy grin.

He is sporting a bright yellow shirt, a polka dot tie, and an orange jacket. The ensemble is eye-blinding and not at all matching, but it seems like it doesn't bother him in the least bit.

When Max asks Violet about it, she laughs. "His outfit is actually pretty tame today. Sunny loves to be fun and unique. He is the resident strategist. With his sunny disposition, his mind is always wandering, but in a good way. He can think of the most creative and unique ways to attack the enemy that no one else can even think of at the drop of a hat."

She steers Max to the next person.

"Garrett," Garrett barely gives Max a fleeting glance before putting his nose back into the book he's reading. Violet smacks the book out of his hand.

"No reading during dinner!" She snaps at him.

Garrett grabs the book off the ground, saves his spot with a leather bookmark and puts it away, much to Violet's happiness.

She turns to Max. "Garrett is the head intelligence officer. In addition to burying his nose in books all day, he also likes to burrow into maps and reports and finding details in them that no one else can."

Violet introduces Max next to a pair of men who looked exactly alike.

"Vick and Valentine are identical twins. But, as you can see, they distinguish themselves by having different style of hair. Vick is the one with black hair and blue highlights, and Valentine has the blue hair with a black highlight. Don't confuse them. They hate it." She whispers the last part under her breath for him.

"Being twins, they work well with one another and are well tuned to each other when in distress. Hence, they do a great job as scouts. If one of them is ever in trouble, the other knows to get help."

Max smiles at the pair who grin back at the same time. They turn toward each other when they realize that they did the same thing at the same time and high-five each other.

She moves on and smiles at a man in all gray. "This is Clay. He's usually in the basement, so you won't see him much except at my dinners. They are all required to attend my dinners."

Clay has very pale skin, but he seems healthy enough. He gives Max a tip of his head in greeting, and Max returns it.

Violet continues. "Clay is the bomb expert. He likes to stay incognito, so he can experiment with his artillery without anyone bothering him. That's best actually. If anyone touches the wrong things, they may accidentally set it off, which is bad for everyone."

She turns to the man sitting next to Clay. "Wolfe, here, takes care of all of the bloodhounds and other animals we keep on the farm. He comes in *real* handy when we need nature to give us a hand, if you know what I mean."

Even though Max doesn't really, the burly man nods at him and he smiles in return. In his time with the underground, he has never seen anyone use an animal in battle before. All he's ever seen are dogs used to sniff out danger and to find people. Perhaps, the rebels have better uses for the animals that he's never seen before.

The next one is a big, hulking man that looks like he can crush Max with one fist.

"We also have Fisher, and like his name, he's our guns and weapons training man."

What does Fisher have to do with weapons? You would think that fishing would be what he does, but that would be too obvious. Perhaps, he sets out baits to lure his enemies or he likes to fish out his victims after he deploys his weapons. Max opens his mouth but is cut off when Violet directs him to his chair.

"Here, sit down. Dinner will be ready in a few minutes." She plops down in her chair opposite him.

Trip is already seated at the head of the table. Max looks around the table curiously. People are being loud and chatty with each other. Sunny is laughing at something while Garrett sits frowning at him as he tries to clean a stain off of his shirt.

Vick and Valentine are arguing about whose chair is who's, even though it does not matter. Clay is nodding at

Wolfe who is talking about his dog and ways that they can use them to blow up the enemy without hurting themselves, and Fisher is staring forlornly at the empty chair next to him.

Max looks at Violet with a questioningly look. "Why's there an empty chair?"

"Oh, that's—

She is cut off when a pair of doors on the other side of the room open, and a bunch of carts are wheeled in by a half a dozen waiters. At the end of the procession, a petite young woman in a chef's hat comes out and waves at all of them before shouting. "Start dishing out the orders, quickly!"

Platters are put on the table to each person's specific desires. Violet leans over during the entire ruckus.

"I hope that you don't mind. I ordered for you. It's the veal parmesan. It's Holloway's best dish. She's our head chef."

Max nods and leans away when a platter is brought down in front of him. The cover is pulled up and shows a delicious looking dish in front of him. His mouth almost starts drooling. The food is fresh and straight from the gardens like Violet said. He hasn't had fresh food since the war began. He smiles at the waiter before digging in when he sees that everyone else is doing the same. Of course, they all have a different meal.

Sunny has steak brightened up with herbs and sauces. Garrett has plain Italian pasta. Vick and Valentine both get cheesy potato soup that is identical to each other.

Clay gets a plate of turkey and mashed potatoes with gravy over both of them. Wolfe has a giant hamburger, and Fisher, well, has fish.

Max looks at Violet and Trip, but they do not have any food in front of them. He does not get the chance to ask because Holloway shoos away the waiters, leaving one cart that has not been opened yet.

"And, for Violet, we have an original recipe!" She brings over one of the platters and opens it to reveal a chunk of lamb mixed with a bunch of spices.

"I made a new dish from my lamb and some of the herbs that you gave me from the garden." Violet grins and digs in as she exclaims, "This is great!"

Holloway turns to Trip and hands him a black bottle. "Here's your drink, like usual. I wish that you'd let me make you something like Violet."

Violet stops eating to comment. "Trip's an old fuddy-duddy. He likes things plain and simple."

Holloway sits down in her seat, and Fisher grins at her. She smiles back and gestures for them to eat.

Max looks curiously at Trip. Violet notices and smiles.

"He doesn't eat anything."

"Really? Doesn't he starve?"

"He looks healthy enough for me."

"What does he drink?"

Violet smiles at him. "Nobody knows."

"Not even the chef?"

Violet is interrupted by a voice from beside him. "The chef's name is Holloway, and I don't think I do, actually."

Max turns around and stares at her with wide eyes. She laughs at his childish face and smiles gently at him. "He just gives me a box of black bottles every month. I hand it out to him once a day."

"Wow, I wonder what it is." He stares at Trip, who is drinking from the bottle. He cannot even tell what color it is.

Holloway follows his gaze and laughs again. "Don't even try to find out." She leans in toward him and whispers, "Yeah, one time, one of my waiters tried to open one of the bottles and suddenly, Trip was there! It was freaky. He didn't even look angry. He just took the bottle from him and put it back in its place. No one ever tried to open another one again."

Violet pulls Max back towards her. "Don't make up stories, Holloway!" Holloway smiles and leans back.

"I'm not! He just showed up out of nowhere! I'm serious!"

"He was just walking by when he saw him, and you know that he doesn't like people messing with his private stuff. Even I don't go near them!"

"Okay! Okay!" Holloway backs away with a friendly sigh and turns toward Fisher. A second later, Violet leans toward his ear and says, "But seriously, don't go near the bottles."

Max nods and proceeds to eat his food. He looks toward Trip's seat only to find that he is not there anymore. He looks around the room, but he just disappeared. Violet notices his awkward staring again. She sighs and says, "He's off and moving again. You'll see him later, in the hallway or something."

He nods and continues eating.

*

Max is shaken awake when the lights are flicked on again. He groans and blinks the sleepiness away from his eyes.

"What time is it?" He looks toward the doorway, expecting to see Violet, but is instead rewarded with the image of Trip. It is hard enough being awakened by the

Warrior, who is apparently a fighting machine that can 'kick all of their butts', according to their boot camp trainer.

It is even harder to be rudely awakened by El Diablo, the legendary man who can survive three life threatening bullets and still kill off so many people. He is more in awe of him than anything else, but it is still a little scary to him.

Trip points at him then points at the hallway behind him. It is pretty obvious that he wants him to come outside. Max gets up and follows him out of the doorway. He is not going to go against Trip. He follows him through the headquarters.

He studies the inside of the buildings as they pass.

Unlike the Legion's headquarters, where the doors were made of the best oak wood and the carpet was genuine fur, the rebel headquarters were mostly bare. It was all either useful or practical.

Trip suddenly grabs his shoulder, and Max stiffens immediately, but it is a false alarm. He just leads him to a room and opens the door. He then points to the door across the room.

Max looks around the room, but he finds that it is just a regular bedroom. He strides over and slowly opens the other door. It is just a bathroom. He turns around and looks at Trip questioningly. What is he trying to tell him here? He opens his mouth and is about to say something when Trip walks over and pulls his arm.

Max stumbles forward and comes to an abrupt stop when he runs into the shower door. Trip gives him a pile of clothes and a towel then walks out of the room, leaving him a little flustered and red-faced.

Is he saying that Max smells or what? He decides not to think too much about it and takes his time reveling in the warmth of the hot spray. It's nice that the guerrillas are giving him a nice room and hot showers – considering that he was just shooting at them not very long ago. When he gets out, he looks at the clothes that are laid out for him.

There is more than just one outfit in the pile. He sees a note on top and snatches it off to read it.

*

To Max,

Hey!! I forced Trip to get you to take a shower! Sorry if you are offended, but honey, you STANK!! These clothes are from me! I got some from Trip as well! He didn't really want to, but hopefully they'll fit you!

Love,

Violet!!!

*

Max has to stifle his laughter when he reads her letter. She is such a clown. He still wonders how the moody Trip can be friends with the excitable Violet. He looks through the pile of clothes. It is an odd mix of bright, neon colors and plain black.

He takes a pair of black jeans, and a bright, checkered blue and white shirt. The jeans are a little long and the shirt's a little tight, but he doesn't look too awkward in the ensemble.

He walks out of the steamy room and into the bedroom. He guesses that this is going to be his new room from now on. According to Violet, that means Trip no longer thinks of him as a threat.

When he turns around, he is surprised to find that Trip is lying on his bed, leaning against the headboard. It is like he is following Max's every move with his eyes. He cannot actually see his eyes behind his hair, but it still feels like he is watching him.

Max holds a hand up lightly. Trip gets up from the bed and walks over to him. He stares at him like a rabbit watching a fox. Trip takes the rest of the clothes from him and opens one of the drawers. He drops them in neatly and stacks them while Max stares on with an open mouth.

Is Trip really cleaning his drawers for him? Before Trip turns around, he quickly shuts his mouth and gives a quick, nervous smile. Trip nods at him before leaving the room. Max sighs and lies down on his bed.

*

It is late at night when a sound stirs Max. He is a little disoriented from his deep slumber until he finds out what woke him. It is the knocking on the door. He gets up and trudges over the door, opening it slowly.

It's Trip. He rubs his eyes and squints at him. "What's wrong?"

"Get dressed." Max sighs and nods okay. He puts on some of the clothes that Violet gave him and opens the door to find Trip waiting for him. He follows him through the hallways until they reach one of the outside doors that he has not seen yet.

Trip steps through the open doorway to show Max into what looks like a ravaged mud pit. There are wooded figures that have targets on them and walls of barbed wire. There are many other things as well that let Max know instantly that this is not going to be a relaxing night for him. He knows he is right when Violet runs out from a door across them with an armful of guns, knives, and various other things.

"What time is it?" He wonders. He can still hear the crickets chirping and owl hooting outside. It cannot be morning already. A glance at Trip's watch tells him he's right.

It is merely 3AM, but to Trip and Violet, there is no time better than the middle of night to start training. This is when the air is the freshest and there is no one to bother them. Even the Legion scouts are generally too sleepy to spy on them at this hour.

Violet stops in front of them, bending down slightly with the weight of the equipment. Max looks up to see Trip walking away.

"Are you ready to rock and roll, rookie?" Violet says with her usual zest.

She drops everything by his feet and says, "OK, show me what you've got!"

He looks through the choices he has as if he was going shopping for a new toy. The pistol captures his attention first. After all, shooting *is* his game. As he picks it up, she chuckles, "Oh, come on, for a sharpshooter, you are going to start with that wimpy thing first?"

As he tries to put it back to make another selection, she grabs his arm and twists it, forcing the weapon out of his hand.

"What did you do that for?" Max asks in shock. His arm is now throbbing in pain.

Shaking her head, she says, "You are obviously not ready. What do you think this is? Kindergarten? I am going to give you another chance. After that, I won't be so easy on you."

Easy? She thinks that was *easy*? Max certainly is not going to wait to find out what she considers to be *not* so easy. Taking a deep breath, he picks up a knife as long as his forearm and says, "Is this one more to your liking?"

Then, he lunges at her with it. Violet easily dodges it by sidestepping and landing a punch to the middle of his chest, forcing him to drop his weapon again. As he hunches over from the pain, he hears giggling. It seems like Violet is enjoying this a little too much.

"Wanna try that again, little man?"

He puts on a pair of brass knuckles and takes a swing at her – missing by a mile.

"This is going to be a long night for you, rookie," Violet says.

Then, she picks up the bullet proof vest and puts it on him.

"Why would I need this? Are you going to shoot me now?" Max asks. In his mind, he's wondering whether he's going to die tonight or not.

"My job is to make sure that you are ready."

All of a sudden, her sunny disposition changes to a deadly serious expression. One look at her sends a cold chill down Max's spine. Yikes! So, *this* is why they call her the Warrior! Before he blinks, she's gone.

"Oh, crap! What is she going to do now?" Max ponders as he starts to hyperventilate a little at the prospect of being shot with a live round any second now. He grabs a gun and ducks behind the first large rock he can find, hoping to buy some time so he can tell where she is.

He listens closely for any signs of disturbance from any direction, but he doesn't sense anything. Then, thud! He falls backwards as a shot hits him on the right corner of his vest. That hurts! He tries to get up and catch his breath. Even though the bullet didn't penetrate his skin, it did knock some wind out of him.

Trying to calm himself down, he tries again. All he can hear this time is the thumping of his own heart in his chest. Everything else has been muted, including all of the loud chirping of the insects. If he thought he was nervous when this little exercise started, he has another thing coming.

Taking another deep breath, he closes his eyes, trying to concentrate. His breathing is slowly becoming more steady and ... Before he can fully calm down, "ouch!" he feels a sharp pain as he looks at his right arm. A dagger has flown by and given him a 6 inch gash, just deep enough to bleed and throb, but not enough to incapacitate him.

He flinches at the gash and hisses. He's going to have to get serious or he's going to be covered in blood before long.

Looking at the mud pit, he has an idea. Earlier, he had stupidly chosen a bright shirt that stood out. Instead of wearing the black shirt from Trip, he chose a red shirt from Violet's selections this morning, not realizing that he needed to camouflage for today's training session. He decides to roll around in the mud and put some on his face. Then, he lies down on the ground behind a tree as motionlessly as he can.

Now that he finds himself in the same position as he would be in as a sharpshooter in the field, he is starting to feel pretty confident. "OK, I am ready, now. Where are you?" Max ponders as he scans for any movement. Before he can find anything, he feels a sharp pain on his back.

"I win!" Violet says cheerfully as she claps her hands like a child. She had driven the scaffold of her dagger into his spine after jumping down from the tree – yes, the same tree that Max is hiding behind.

"Well, that was fun!" Violet exclaims while Max groans a little as he nurses his wounds.

"Don't worry, that portion of the training is over – for today anyways," Violet explains. "We always give you three chances to come back. The person who gets three solid shots in wins."

Patting him on the shoulder, "Don't worry. You did well – for your first try, anyways. It's really just for us to gauge how good you are so we know how much training you need."

"So, how do you think I did?" Max asks, not really sure if he wants to hear the answer.

"As well as I expected." Violet says diplomatically. Then, she leads him to the mud pit with the barbed wires and says with a smile, "Since you are already covered in mud, I think we should start with this one."

For the next few hours, Violet puts him through drill after drill until the sun comes up.

"OK, I think that is good for now." Violet says.

Max slumps in relief. He has never been so glad to hear eight little words before. He instantly falls on the ground as he catches his breath. That seems like something that he's going to be doing a lot of from now on.

"No, no, no, you never lie down after an extraneous exercise, no matter how exhausted you are. Get up. We need to clean you up and put some food in you. After that little workout, you should be famished! I'm hungry just watching you work." Violet says teasingly.

Now that she mentions it, Max finally thinks about his stomach. He is hungry and thirsty. The only taste in his mouth is mud, not exactly his favorite flavor.

*

"So, what do you think?" Violet asks.

"I think you were right," Trip responds, knowing that she has been dying to hear those words for some time and that she is going to gloat. Before he can finish his thought, Violet expectedly shouts, "Yeah!! Told you so!"

Trip and Violet have been watching Max for some time now. It didn't take them long to figure out that Max and Thom are best friends and that Max is not too crazy about the prospect of being in the Legion. Hence, they have known for some time now that Max may be the key to winning this war against the Legion.

The problem is Trip has never liked the idea of having to use deceit to win anything. As far as he is concerned, the righteous one should be the one who prevails and succeeds in the end – no matter how long it takes.

Violet, on the other hand, doesn't see this as deception, simply shrewd strategy. From the very beginning, she promised Trip that she wouldn't force anyone in the Desiderios to do anything against their wishes, including Max.

If he chooses to betray his childhood friend, that would be his decision. If he chooses not to, they completely understand. She plans on keeping that promise. In all of the years that she has known Trip, she has never broken one before and she does not intend on starting now. Convinced that Violet is a woman of her word, Trip trusts that she knows what she is doing.

Trip was watching Max's morning training session. While he knows that Max has a lot of work to do, he is impressed at the speed that he is learning. From what he has seen, Max seems to be a very quick learner. His small size is not even an issue. In fact, his tiny frame allows him to crawl through the barbed wires faster than most of the other men.

He is also able to evade potential hazards much easier. With his speed and intelligence, he can be a valuable asset to his team regardless of whether or not he is willing to infiltrate the Legion for them.

*

After having cleaned himself up, Max emerges from his room wearing all black. As he sits down at the table to join Trip, Violet, and the rest of the group for breakfast, Violet says, "Hey, look, Trip, I think you are about to get a protégé!"

The men begin to tease Max. While some ruffles his hair as he walks by, others cheer.

"Watch out! Before long, he will be asking for Trip's mystery drink at the dinner table!" Sunny couldn't resist.

Always needing to have the last word, Garrett replies, "As if he's willing to share! Trip's drink makes him superhuman, didn't you know!"

"Alright, alright, calm down, everybody. I want everyone to know that he has passed his first day here with us!" Violet announces.

"Congratulations, rookie!" Holloway says as she gives him a big heaping helping of scrambled eggs. "Eat up!"

As Max gobbles down his breakfast, Wolfe teases, "Hey, easy there before you choke to death! We can't lose you on the first day! I thought I was the biggest eater here, but looks like you are going to give me a run for my money on the title soon."

Max blushes and slows down a little. Violet smiles. She is glad that everyone is taking him in so readily. Even though this is only his second day here, it seems like he has always been part of the family. Trip, on the other hand, has a solemn look on his face. Violet wonders what he is thinking, but has a pretty good idea.

*

"Hey, are you alright?" Violet asks.

"Yeah, why wouldn't I be?" Trip answers flatly.

"Well, you stayed at the table longer than usual, for one thing."

Even though she is trying to tease him with her response, there is a bit of seriousness in it. After all, Trip never stays anywhere longer than he needs to. The fact that he did means that he was there for a reason.

"Just wanted to be sure."

"So, are you?" Violet asks curiously.

"Not yet."

"Why not?"

"His soul is too pure."

"Are you saying that he is not willing to help us?"

"He's his best friend," Trip says as if he is asking her whether or not she would be willing to betray their friendship.

"I know what you are thinking. This is different."

"How?"

"We have a darn good cause." Violet says lightheartedly, trying to ease the tension a little.

"That may be true, but someone like him is not going to compromise his principles for someone else's cause."

"Well, you know that's not true." Violet says as her mood shifts to a more serious tone. "So, what's your plan now?"

"Not sure yet."

"I think we should just go ahead and tell him."

"What would that accomplish? He is not ready to hear it."

"How can you tell?"

"It's too much for one person to take in after what you put him through today."

Violet grins and replies, "Good point."

Chapter 5: Best Friends

The best place to find someone is to start with their last known location. "If I were Max, where would I be?" Thom ponders as he surveys the battlefield. He walks along the area where the sharpshooters were, hoping to find something, anything, that can help him connect with his friend. After all of these years together, he figures he should have a sort of a sixth sense that can help him.

As he paces back and forth, he is disappointed that he has not found anything worthwhile. Except for a lot of footprints. "Great, it would have been great if I paid more attention to the tracking portion of the training." Most of the prints look like they came from the same type of boots and there are a lot of them. It appears the entire sharpshooter squadron was here, trampling the grass and breaking branches.

Even to a relatively untrained eye, it is obvious that they were not trying to hide their whereabouts. Instead, they were trying to get a comfortable hiding place to settle down. There are also a lot of smudges that seem to have been caused by different body parts when they knee or lie down for their shot. There are even more that trampled over the previous set when they came back to look for Max after he was reported missing.

Because the battle ended abruptly, there were no casualties on either side. So, it appeared that all of that shuffling and positioning was not very fruitful. Nevertheless, he crouches down to see which spot would give him the best advantage over the enemies. That would be where Max was. After all, he is the best. After re-positioning himself a few times, he decides on a place that is almost completely covered by the trees, but angled up so he can get a clear shot and low enough where the enemy would not expect him to hide. In his experience, most snipers like to come from the top rather than the bottom, so they can get a bird's eye view.

For the next few minutes, he looks at the landscape from the sniper's view. "Wow, he could have done a lot of damage if he wanted," Thom thinks to himself in amazement. He can see everything from here, including a full view of the streets in both directions and all of the windows in the nearby buildings, where the action was the heaviest. Yet, Max did not kill anyone. For all he knows, he probably didn't even fire a shot. If he did, hopefully, it was not against his own men.

Then, Thom shifts his attention to the hideout spot itself. Max may have accidentally dropped some clues. But as he looks around, all he sees are government-issued shells, around a half a dozen total. It's useless information.

All it tells him is that Max shot at some people, and Thom isn't even sure if Max had shot at their own people or the guerillas. He sighs and keeps looking.

Just when he is about to give up, something catches his eye, a small black feather. "Hum, interesting, which kind of bird would have left this small piece of feather on the ground?"

He still remembers the days when he would look out the window and sees blue jays chasing after one another in spring and the days when the squirrels hopped across his backyard eating ripe pieces of peaches and pecans that fell off the trees during the summer.

Since the war began, many of the trees have been destroyed, taking with them the homes of these critters, forcing most of them to flee the area.

Nowadays, the most common birds he sees are the vultures that pick at dead bodies and the most often seen animals are the rats that scavenge and spread diseases from the corpses.

Sad, really.

He wishes things could go back to the way they're meant to be. He wishes that Max was by his side and everyone was happy.

"This is all the rebels' fault! When will they ever give up this war? Why are they so insistent on taking down the Legion? What have we ever done to them?" Thom ponders as he shakes his head.

He studies the feather that he's holding in his hand, comparing it to what he was taught about birds. From what he knows, the color of the feather doesn't look like it came from a vulture. It might have come from a crow, but the texture is too soft to be one. It looks like it may have come from a water fowl, like a black swan, but where is there a swan in this part of the world? He takes out a small bag that he brought just for the occasion and places the feather in it. He hopes that he may find more clues later.

Then, he notices a set of footprints that seem to be heading a different direction than the others and appear to be deeper, too, which is definitely worth a closer look. Is this a heavy person who left this print or is this a regular man who is carrying something heavy? Out of the entire sharpshooting team, there is not a single person who may be considered overweight. So, if these prints were made by a heavy man, he is definitely not one of them. None of the sharpshooters were carrying heavy machinery. The only things they usually carry are their rifles, ammunition, and a canteen, about 50 pounds. They have a heavy load, but these tracks are far too deep for a man merely carrying supplies. It's more likely that the tracks were made by a man with the weight of two.

It's not only the deepness of the tracks that intrigues Thom. The steps that he follows also appear to be shorter than the average man's stride, almost as though a person was limping or struggling under a heavy load.

A glimmer of hope returns to Thom, "Maybe Max was kidnapped!" Despite what he has read in the journal, Thom is still hopeful that his friend has been forced to be on the rebels' side. There is just no way he could be doing it willingly. As he follows the trail of the footsteps, they disappear behind the trees.

He uses what he can of his meager tracking skills in order to follow the trail, but it's not long before he loses sight of the path made by the person.

"Darn it! Now, where did he go?" Thom looks for any sign of disturbance in the forest. Then, he sees something hanging on a tree – a small piece of cloth. He picks it off and rubs it gently. It's the same texture and style as the standard Legion uniform, a loose, dark colored fabric. It could be Max's.

"Now I know that I'm following the right lead at least." As he continues down the same way for awhile, he comes out on the other end of the grove into a poor slum area. It's full of trash and dung left on the ground. He can see many, dirty people milling around, probably waiting for someone to come by, so they can steal from them.

"Ugh!" Disgusting! It smelled horrible, like something or someone had died right then and there.

It's impossible to find a trail here. There's simply too many people and debris left around. He would never find anything this way.

Frustrated, he heads back to the Legion headquarters.

*

Knock, knock. Max hears two quick bangs on the door. He opens it and isn't surprised when he sees Violet standing there.

"Hiya, rookie! How are you feeling?"

"Good."

"Now that you are more relaxed, what do you think?"

"About what?"

"Anything. Since you have been here, you haven't really asked any questions. I am assuming that you have many, but are just too shy to ask. Maybe you are afraid that *El Diablo* will rip your head off if you do." Violet says teasingly.

"Well, the thought has come to my mind." Max says with a grin.

"Look at that! You are becoming more and more like one of us every time I see you!"

Max opens the door further and motions for her to enter the room. She bounces in before plopping down on his bed. Cocking her head, she smiles at him.

"So? Is there anything you want to know?"

"Well, of course!"

"Fire away! No pun intended, of course. Hehe."

"Okay…," Max isn't sure if he wants to ask this, but he decides to barrel ahead and asks, "Why me?"

"Why not you? You are good at what you do, aren't you?"

"Thanks, but so are many others."

"Not as good as you."

Max is not convinced that the answer is the truth, not the full truth anyways, but he is not going to press. "Okay, why did Trip have to kidnap me from the field?"

"It's the fastest way. It's easier than trying to figure out where you were. We started this battle because we knew you were going to be there. You should be honored that we put in so much effort – just for *you*!" Violet says as she pokes him lightly on the forehead.

"That's kind of a big risk to take for one person, isn't it?"

"Oh, you are so worth it!" Violet jests. "But, no, not really. We selected that location so that we knew where the sharpshooters would be and the risk was minimal for our men. I would never put them in undue danger. We are a family! In any case, as expected, you were right where we predicted you would be."

"Does it not bother you that I worked for the Legion?"

"Ah, now the real question starts... No, we know you don't actually work for them."

"How?"

"Come on, now. If Trip and I didn't know your work with the underground, we can't really call ourselves the leaders of this operation, can we?"

"Yes, but how do you know that I didn't defect and change sides? After all, I was pointing my rifle at your men."

Violet becomes serious for a second and says, "We also know your true intentions."

At the sound of those words, Max panics a little. How would they know what his intentions are? He's never discussed it with anyone. Well, he did write a little bit about it in his journal, but no one was allowed to read it. Have they been spying on him?

As always, it feels as though Violet can read his mind when she says, "Relax, we didn't read your journal."

Uh huh, so she does know about his journal.

"You know, there is a fine line between espionage and invasion of privacy. We have our limits when it comes to invading other people's personal space." Violet says jokingly. "The truth of the matter is we don't need to read it to know. You're pretty much an open book. Actually, you seem to wear your emotions on your sleeves."

"Am I really that obvious?"

"Oh, yeah. Even a child can tell."

"So, if you don't mind my asking, what do you think are my true intentions?"

"Don't believe me, huh? OK, I will tell you. You believe your parents worked for us before their disappearance and you want to know what happened to them. You know that they must have believed in our cause for them to have committed themselves to us. So, you joined the underground hoping to find out more, but no one knows. Even though you haven't gotten any closer and you have had frictions with some of the men, you are not going to give up your search."

Max blushes at hearing the exact truth out of her mouth. She knows everything already.

He looks down on the ground as he thinks about his parents. It has been almost five years since he last saw them and he misses them so much. Knowing that expression on his face, Violet stops talking to give him a minute to collect himself as she flashes an understanding smile.

After he lifts his head back up, she asks, "Do you have any other questions?"

"Yes," Max asks softly, "Do you know what happened to them?"

His eyes are beaming with anticipation, hoping that the answer is a good one, but fearing the worst. He is not sure if he wants to know, but he has to. Violet wants to tell him something that will be of some comfort to him, but the truth is anything but.

"Yes," Violet answers solemnly. Max looks back down on the floor again. He knows what that means. They must be dead. He tries to hold back a tear from dropping from his eyes, but one escapes anyways. He wipes it quickly and discreetly, hoping she didn't see it.

"I'm sorry," Violet continues. "Do you really want to know?"

"Yes," he answers even softer than before.

"The Legion killed them." She says before pausing for a moment to see if he stops her. When he doesn't, she continues.

"Your mother was part of our intelligence team, and your father was our bomb expert. The last report we received from her was on December 6, 2086. She told us that General Hawk was her new inside contact in the Legion headquarters and that she was en route to meet with him. When she did not come back the next day, your father went searching for her. The following day, we found both of their bodies floating in the river. We recovered and buried them."

Max cannot believe his ears. He already knew that his parents were most probably dead, but he didn't realize how much harder it was to hear his suspicions confirmed. It feels like he's been hit by a ton of bricks. All of this time, he hoped that they were in a super secret mission and could not contact him for fear of revealing themselves or putting him in danger.

"How did they die?"

"They were both shot execution style."

Max cringes at her words. Suddenly, the image of his parents being tied to a post and summarily shot flashes before his eyes and a chill goes down his spine.

"Was it a quick death?"

"Are you sure you want to know?"

Ugh! Not again! When Violet says those words, it's never good news.

He shakes his head and says, "Can I see them?"

"Of course. For their and your protection, their graves are not marked, but we know where each of our fallen comrades are buried."

She gestures for him to follow her as she walks out of his room and takes him outside the building. She pulls up a dark van, and Max gets in the passenger seat, wondering exactly where she is taking him.

He zones out, staring at nothing, as he tries to get over the shock of this news. He couldn't believe it.

It's not until Violet pulls into a familiar driveway that he starts to pay attention to where they'd been heading.

Wait a minute. This is his family's estate. He'd know his home from anything even if he was blindfolded.

Violet shifts into park at the back of the house. "We are here. I will give you a minute."

"What? Here?"

Max cannot believe he is standing in his family's graveyard in the back of the estate. All this time, he never knew that his parents were already buried here. But, it's almost impossible to tell where they were buried.

Sensing his confusion, Violet walks by and says, "If you look carefully, there are two graves marked by large stones. By each of the stones, we planted a flower that represents the person buried in some form. It may be their favorite color or scent. Or, it may be something that represents their character or hometown. Only those who know them would understand the significance. We do this for all of our fallen comrades."

"Thank you."

Max looks for the stone and sees a sprig of lilac. "That must be Mom." His mother always loved this seemingly insignificant plant. She loved the small petals, which look minuscule alone, but emit such a calm and relaxing aroma.

Then, he looks at the space on the left side to hers and finds another large stone hidden in the base of a sunflower. "That must be Dad." He was like a ray of sunshine, always cheerful and upbeat, no matter what was happening. Without him, everything seems so dim and lifeless.

Max is thankful that the Desiderios was kind enough to bring them home. He is also comforted by the thought that his parents are now at peace and have each other for company in the afterlife. They have always loved one another very deeply.

After paying his respects, he looks at Violet and says, "Thank you" again.

"I am sorry for your loss," Violet says, knowing that there is really nothing she can say to make him feel better.

*

Returning to the rebel headquarters, Trips says, "How did it go?"

"As can be expected," Violet answers.

"Has he made the connection yet?"

"No, but he's coming around pretty quickly. Are you sure we cannot just tell him the truth?"

"No, he needs to figure it out by himself. Otherwise, he would not be able to commit to our cause wholeheartedly."

"I know, but it's just gut wrenching having to watch him go through all that."

"You know it would be much worse for him if you dump it all on him at once."

"I guess."

*

Max is trying to get a grip of what he has learned and felt since he arrived at the rebel headquarters. It almost seems like he should know more or feel more, but he doesn't. He doesn't know what he should be doing. Lying on his bed, he is more frustrated than ever before. Who is this General Hawk? Did he meet him with Thom? Was he the one who murdered his parents? If so, why? What was he after?

Then, a darker thought comes to mind, one that he has been avoiding since his parent's disappearance, but one that he must face. Was Thom involved in his parents' death? How much does he know? Judging from the cheerfulness in his face the last time that he saw him, he prays that his best friend has nothing to do with his parents' death. It would be the ultimate betrayal. He wouldn't be able to handle it. He does not know what he would do if Thom was involved in any way.

Then again, as the commanding officer, how can Thom *not* know? Even though he was not the sharpest student in school, he is no fool. He usually picks up things pretty quickly. As the General of the Legion, you would think that he knows what is happening among his own men. If he does not know, that means someone else is pulling the strings behind the scenes. If that is the case, whoever this is must be very dangerous.

*

Thom enters the Legion's headquarters on foot. He can see the guards standing on the roof and by the gate. He gives them a nod before entering the empty hall.

He doesn't usually mind the loudness that his footsteps make when he's walking through, but now, it seems unusually lonely.

He's almost to his private hall when a soldier comes up to him.

"General Thomas, I have some documents for you to look at."

The soldier hands them to him, and he waves him off afterwards.

However, as soon as he enters his room, he drops the papers on the ground and opens Max's journal to continue reading.

*

February 14, 2087

It's Valentine's Day. Even though it's not really a holiday, I always look forward to this day of the year. Mom always took the time to bake heart shaped cookies and Dad always brought home flowers — lilacs to be exact, Mom's favorite. There was always so much love here at my parent's estate, but not this year.

Just like Christmas, it is empty. There is no one here but me. I continue to keep the house nice and neat, hoping that one day they will return. Even though I have been keeping up with the yard work, the flowers just do not bloom as beautifully as they used to. Mom always had the green thumb, which I apparently did not inherit.

I wonder how Thom is doing. The last I heard, he just finished boot camp and is now a full-fledged soldier. He sounds so happy. I didn't tell him how lonely it is here because I don't want to burst his bubble.

*

As he reads more of Max's journal, Thom feels worse and worse about himself. How in the world could he have been so self-absorbed not to see any of the signs? He was going on and on about his own life and not once has he thought about how Max was *really* doing. He just assumed that he was happy because he had nothing to complain about. That was a dumb assumption!

In a way, Thom is starting to wonder if Max did leave the journal for him to find. Perhaps, he thought no one else would care enough about him to look through his things. Looking at the words, it just seems that Max wants him to know that he was hurt by his insensitivity without coming out and saying it. That would be Max, alright – a little sensitive guy who acts like everything is fine.

"So, what have I learned so far?" Thom lists out the items in his head. First, he goes to his parents' estate quite often. Second, he is working for the Desiderios, but does not like the people because they hate him. Third, he hates the Legion. Fourth, he is a sharpshooter and a mechanic. Fifth, he would like to remain anonymous.

"So, if we put all of these things together, where would Max be? Think, think, think! Ah! Nothing…" The only thing Thom can think of to do now is to search his parents' estate.

He hides the journal and heads out once more.

It's been a while since he's been there – the Sullivan Estate. When he was young, he would come by all the time to play with Max.

Even though the estate is large, it's very much like home. In a way, it's more like home to him than his house. Every time he dropped by there was always something baking in the kitchen. Mr. and Mrs. Sullivan always made him feel very welcome.

Max's parents were so trusting of him that they gave him a spare key in case he was ever in the neighborhood and just wanted to come in and take a load off. He rarely had to use this key before. Usually, when he wanted to come in, all he had to do was knock on the door and someone would be home to greet him with a cheerful smile.

Thom sighs as he remembers what the Sullivan family used to be like.

*

The Sullivans were the quintessential couple. They met one another when they were studying together in the local University where he studied Chemistry and she studied Political Science. They have not been apart ever since.

To anyone who has ever met them, they were loving and caring, not just to one another, but to everyone they have ever met.

If they saw a homeless person, they never hesitated to give them what they could – whether it was money or food. Max's father Philip was also known to give away the coat he was wearing if it was a cold day.

That is not to say that Max's mother Sonya would not do the same. Whenever she tried to, however, her husband would stop her because, like Max, she was small in size and not in the best of health.

Some may even consider her frail. If there was a sickness going around, she usually would catch it. On the other hand, she's no pushover either.

Where she lacked in physical strength, she made up for in intelligence.

Philip was an easy going scientist who was always at the top of his class. He was one of those who never needed to study but aced all of his exams.

Not having to study left Philip a lot of time to do other things, ranging from partying to helping others in need, which made him an immensely popular man on campus. As far as their friends were concerned, they're the same today as the first day they met.

They married as soon as they graduated from college. It didn't take Philip long to land a job as the head researcher for the government. Because of the sensitivity of his projects, he would never discuss his work with his family, but that did not stop him from doing some extra experimenting and researching at home.

During the first year of their marriage, Max came into their lives. Even though Sonya was also in the top of her class, she wanted to be there for her baby boy every step of the way from day one. She would use every experience as an opportunity to teach her son without making it sound like school. When she saw flowers, she would explain to him different parts of a plant from root to the petal and how to take care of them.

When she met rude people, she taught him how to remain calm and rational.

Thom has always wanted a mother as nurturing as Sonya. Even though he had a good mother, his home was not the same.

Even though his mother was always home, his father was the exact opposite. His mother knew that Thom missed his father quite a bit, especially during holidays and special occasions, and tried to compensate by showering him with a great deal of the latest gadgets and toys.

Of course, even he knew that that was more out of guilt than anything else and could never replace love, but as a child, he certainly wasn't complaining.

When other children in school brought their fathers in during career days, he was always envious of them. Those children always looked so happy to be with their fathers as they dragged them into the classroom and proudly announced their father's titles and told everyone how their fathers are the best in the world.

Even though he was sure that he was the one with the best father in the world, he could not possibly tell anyone else that because he was never able to bring his father into the classroom. He hated the fact that he couldn't. His father was never around long enough for him to take him anywhere. He also never answered any questions regarding his job.

Despite the seemingly loving relationship that Victor assumes that he has with his son, Thom has always felt a distance from his father.

For one thing, Victor was already 40 years old by the time Thom was born. It was only after Thom ascended to the ranks of General that he even learned what his father does for a living.

Even now, he is still not allowed to enter his father's office without being announced first. At least now he knows how his parents live in a house that is even bigger than the Sullivan's. But, who is competing?

*

Today, Thom knocks on the door as always, hoping that it'll open and Max will be there, but as he waits for what seems like an eternity, no one comes to the door. Disappointed, he uses the key to let himself in. The house is not the same as he remembers it. Even though every piece of furniture is in place and all of the artwork and decorations remain, it feels completely empty.

There are no freshly baked goods coming from the kitchen. There are no sounds of laughter. The birds that used to frequent the gardens on the estate also seem to be missing.

Putting aside the hollow feeling, he walks through the house looking for signs of life or at least a clue as to Max's whereabouts. Alas, he cannot find anything. The entire house is spotless, as if someone has just come by to clean it. There is not a piece of trash, scrap paper, or dirt anywhere. The books are nicely placed on the bookshelves. The dishes are in the cabinet where they belong. Every article of clothing is neatly hung in the closet. Even the beakers in the laboratory are clean and neatly placed on the shelves.

Ordinarily, a clean house in a large estate does not seem that unusual. After all, rich people often have maids who come in regularly to make sure that everything is tidy.

But, in the Sullivans' case, it does send up a red flag. Max's family has never liked to hire help. If they have the time, they prefer to do things themselves.

It's good for the soul, Mr. Sullivan would always say.

So, if Max has been missing for three days and his parents have been missing for quite some time now, who exactly is cleaning up this place in their absence? As far as he knows, there are no known relatives who live close enough to swing by and do housework.

Being prepared, Thom takes out his kit, so he can capture any fingerprints for analysis. Perhaps someone had been inside to clean the house.

Surprisingly, he cannot find a single print, which is definitely suspicious. Being a home, there should at least be prints of the owners somewhere.

No maid is ever *that* meticulous. It seems whoever cleaned the house also made sure that all of the prints have been wiped.

Thom is now worried for his friend. First, he disappears. Then, his home is wiped clean. He is becoming convinced that Max has been kidnapped and the assailants are covering their tracks so no one can ever find him again. Knowing how the Legion treats their captives, he is hoping that Max is not being imprisoned somewhere. Being as small as he is, he is afraid that his friend will not be able to handle it.

Thom puts on a pair of gloves and starts to look under rugs and furniture, behind books and closets, above shelves and ceiling, and into vases and drawers for any clues or signs of struggle. Even though he feels somewhat guilty for invading the Sullivans' privacy, he convinces himself that this is to help rescue his best friend. He is not about to let anything slip by him, no matter how insignificant it may be.

After hours of a long and scrutinizing search, he comes across a loose board under the bed in the master bedroom. He pries it open and is not sure what to think. Underneath the floor are rifles and handguns along with thousands of rounds of ammunition. As far as he knows, the Sullivans are all peace loving pacifists.

Why in the world would they have so many weapons hiding in here? Do they even know how to use them? Even if they don't, they must be hiding them for someone or for some reason.

Either case, it seems that Max's sweet parents are or were leading a double life. Is that what Max is doing too? Is he a double agent who works for both the Legion and the Desiderios?

In the corner of the secret compartment, he sees something even more intriguing – two identical notebooks, both of which are plain black and look very old and worn. He quickly flips through both of them and instantly realizes that he has found what he was looking for. After all, why would anyone hide notebooks with so much artillery underneath their bed? They must have something very important to say in them.

"Hm, looks like journal writing runs in the family," Thom thinks aloud.

Looking at the clock, he realizes that it is getting late. If he stays any longer, the Legion will come looking for him and he certainly does not want them involved until he finds out more for himself. Thom closes the floor board and quickly makes his way back to the headquarters.

He is hopeful that he will soon be able to solve the mysterious disappearances. With so much writing, he is bound to find out who their associates are and where they go. They cannot possibly just disappear from the face of the earth without a single trace. Somebody must know something.

Chapter 6: Lost Childhood

As Thom opens the first notebook, he sees it is full of chemical formulas and engineering designs. It definitely does not look like the same type of journal entries that Max is keeping. This looks more like Philip Sullivan's notes from the laboratory. What exactly has he been experimenting that needs to be hidden under the floor board? He knows that Philip worked for the government. Perhaps, it was his way of keeping sensitive projects secret.

Then, he looks through the second one. As expected, this one is Sonya Sullivan's journal. This one is much more informal and resembles that of Max's. There are pages and pages of entries written in chronological order going back many years. The last entry was written on December 6, 2086.

*

December 6, 2086

It's such a beautiful day today! There is a light snow flurry coming down but the sky is gorgeous and the air is so crisp and fresh. Max always loves the way the snow falls on his tongue. It's the cutest thing! I hope he is doing well at school. He has always been such a good boy. He's my sweet little angel.

I'm meeting a new friend today. His name is John. We are meeting by the old church in town. That church is stunning. It has such beautiful statues and artwork. He wants to introduce me to his other friends. There are about 12 of them. I don't know anything about them right now, besides the fact that they always have a get together every Friday morning at 10AM. I hope they are nice! I would love to have nice friends over for dinner sometime!

*

That's interesting. Even though her writing seems to indicate a casual meeting, it is pretty obvious that it is anything but. If it's the old church that Thom is thinking of, it's in rubbles and continues to fall apart every day. It is no place for sightseeing. Nevertheless, that is the only one that he can think of that used to be beautiful. It is about a 20 mile drive from the Sullivan estate to the old church. Under normal circumstances, this does not appear to be unusual, but in time of war, this is a long and dangerous way to go to meet a simple friend.

Who is this friend John anyways? Is he a member of the Legion or the Desiderios? Or, is he completely unrelated to either side? Considering that Mrs. Sullivan is meeting someone that far away on slippery roads, it is most probably not the latter. The problem is John is a popular name in these parts.

It could be anyone. Another problem is – who is to say that John is his real name?

Considering that this is the last entry in this journal, Thom fears that John has something to do with Mrs. Sullivan's disappearance. Worse, his gut tells him that the Sullivans are no longer alive, but he has to hold out some hope that they still are, even if the chances are slim. He has not seen either of Max's parents for a very long time. In fact, it has been so long that he does not recall the last time that he even saw them.

Thom decides to go back to the beginning of the notebook and start from there instead. The first entry goes back to July 12, 2073.

Isn't that the day that Max was born? So, she probably started this journal as a tribute to her little boy.

*

July 12, 2073

I am shaking as I write this. Today, the world is perfect! My little angel has finally made his long awaited entrance to the world. I cannot be happier! He is absolutely gorgeous with his ten chubby fingers and ten chubby toes. His chunky little rosy cheeks complement his huge brown eyes and little fluffy golden hair so beautifully. I simply cannot get enough of him!

Philip is ecstatic, too! He has not stopped gushing about his new addition to the family to everyone he sees or talks to since he cut the little angel's cord. He is showering him with so many kisses that I think the little angel is getting a little annoyed! □

*

As Thom reads those words, a small part of him becomes a little jealous of his best friend. He wonders what his own parents thought of on the day that he was born. If memory serves, his father wasn't even in the hospital that day. As always, he was away at work.

It's kind of sad to know that work is more important to your father than your own birth, especially when you are his only child. He sighs.

Well, nothing can be changed about that. Let's see what else Mrs. Sullivan gushes about.

*

July 15, 2073

My poor Max! He has a terrible case of colic and no matter what I do; I cannot seem to ease his pain. I wish I can do more to help him, but the doctor says there really isn't anything else we can do. All I can do is hold him tight and hope that it comforts him.

*

Again, a tingle of jealousy works its way through his mind.

When Thom was a child, his mother was always at home, but was not the one who would take care of him. She played the role of the perfect hostess who was always prim and proper who greeted her husbands' guests with the utmost decorum. Even though she brought him out to meet the guests quite often, it was more to show him off than anything else. After the meet and greet sessions were over, he was usually left alone again.

It was his nanny who did most of the childrearing, to use that word loosely. What was her name again...? Oh, that's right. It was old Mrs. Taylor. She was a strict and mean biddy. He was not allowed to make any kind of a mess at all. Even as a toddler, he was expected to stay clean. That usually meant that he was not allowed to go out and play with the other kids. Instead, he would look out the window and wish that he was with them.

He was also expected to address and greet his elders, including his parents, formally when he saw them, calling them ma'am and sir instead of mommy and daddy like other children of his age. He never cared for that, but did it anyways because he was expected to do so. Otherwise, he would be confined to his room the next day with nothing but bread and water as punishment.

Mrs. Taylor also made sure that he was studying or learning something at all times. When he first learned to crawl, she wanted him to walk. When he began to walk, she expected him to start riding a bicycle. When he figured out how to hold a pencil, she expected him to write the alphabets. It was always one thing or another.

Eventually, he became so tired of learning all the time that he lost all desire to study. Instead, he would find ways to sneak out. To make sure that he was not caught, however, he was always careful not to let anyone see him, which means he stayed away from other children. He also had identical changes of clothes ready so he would still be spotless when he came back.

It wasn't until kindergarten when he met Max that he started playing with other children. At first, he felt very awkward, not knowing how to approach anyone. Max was the first one to introduce himself and made him feel welcome. Ever since then, he has been his best and most enduring friend, which he sincerely hopes is still true today.

If it was not for Max, he might have become a hermit, albeit a highly intelligent and talented one, who was afraid of people rather than the confident general that he is today.

Thom reads through the next few entries. They are filled with Max's childhood milestones – when he took his first step, lost his first tooth, said his first word, etc. Each entry is full of the same loving and tender words. Before long, he starts to scan through them quickly. He's not sure which feeling is stronger – boredom from the monotony of the words or guilt from invading his best friend's privacy.

After all, there is a limit to how much sweetness a guy can take. At the same time, he really hopes to find a clue somewhere in the notebook that can help his friend. As he contemplates putting the notebook away, Thom sees an entry that looks interesting. It's about the first day that the Sullivans met him.

Even though this entry probably will not shed any more light on any of the Sullivans' whereabouts, he wants to read it. He tries to justify reading it to himself. After all, most people would be curious as to how others really see them and what better way to find out than to read it from their private journal? Yes, the sense of guilt is beginning to get stronger every second, but he cannot help himself.

*

September 30, 2078

Max is having a great time at school. He met this boy called Thom. He thinks he's a little shy, but he really likes him after he got to know him. At first, he wasn't sure if he should approach him since he was always sitting by himself, not talking to anyone, but once Max introduced himself, this boy Thom seems to have warmed up to him.

He was going on and on about how funny this boy is, not in a ha-ha way, but just everything he says makes him laugh. It's kind of hard to explain. And, he cannot stop talking about how great of an artist he is, either. He said his new friend drew a picture of him and it was really silly. He has a really big head, big ears, and big eyes, but it kind of looks like him. I guess he was drawing a caricature. Max does have a big head, large ears, and even bigger eyes. It looks so cute on him though! He seems to really enjoy this boy's company. I hope they can stay friends. I would love to meet him some day. He sounds like such a sweet boy!

*

Thom is happy that Mrs. Sullivan had only good things to say about him, but then again, like the rest of the entries, even this one is sweet. "Is Mrs. Sullivan capable of getting mad about anything or anyone?" Thom asks himself.

As he continues to flip through the pages, another one catches his eye. It is the day that his parents met Max's parents. That is a story that he does not really know. All he remembers is that one day Max told him that his parents would love to invite his parents over for dinner since they were best friends, but he doesn't know what their parents think of one another.

If this entry was written about anyone else, he could care less and would have breezed through it like so many of the others, but considering that his father is the head of the Legion and Max is a member of the rebellion, how the relationship between their parents began may be important to shed some light on why the two families went their separate ways later.

*

July 3, 2079

Max's birthday is coming up and he is really excited! We bought all of the presents that he asked for. I didn't realize there are so many versions of the same toys that he asks for over and over again. I guess it's almost like how some women can have 10 different pairs of red pumps, but thinks each is different because of the slight variety of the shades, like cherry versus crimson. It seems to be the new fad this year. I see lots of children on the playground with them.

He also invited ten of his best friends. He asked us three times to make sure that Thom is invited. That silly boy! Of course, we would invite his best friend. In fact, we did one better. We invited Thom's parents for dinner last night. They also seem like shy people, kind of like the impression that Max had of Thom when they first met. I guess it runs in the family. Once they started talking, though, they seemed nice.

Amelia is so courteous and polite. I feel like I was talking to a member of the royalty sometimes! She brought the best tasting chocolate soufflés that I have ever tasted. Yum! But, for some reason, she kept changing the subject when I asked her for her recipe. I guess it's a family secret or something and she didn't want to be rude by not sharing.

Victor is also very proper and formal. He hardly moved from his seat at the table during dinner. He had the etiquette of a school headmaster. His head was so poised and his back completely straight when seated. He also never spoke with his mouth full. But then again, he hardly spoke at all. When he finally moved to go to the sofa after eating, he barely moved from that spot until it was time to leave. Of course, that is not to say that he was not friendly or anything. I think he just needs time to warm up to new people.

I hope we get to meet them again soon! I would love to get to know them better. After all, if my Max is going to be best friends with little Thom, we should get to be best friends with them, too.

*

Thom chuckles when he reads this entry. Mrs. Sullivan gives his parents way too much credit. The reason his mother was not willing to share the recipe is because she didn't know it. As the governess Mrs. Taylor was usually the one in the kitchen. Mother only tells her what she would like for her to prepare for each meal and Mrs. Taylor takes care of the rest. That is not to say that she did everything around the house. On the contrary, she often never did much. She always ordered the lower servants to do the menial work like cleaning.

Unlike the Sullivans, Thom's parents have a lot of hired help. In addition to Mrs. Taylor, there are three cooks, one butler, two gardeners, and numerous maids. Every one of them is constantly busy doing different chores. Sometimes

Thom wonders if they are actually doing things that need to be done.

For example, he often sees the maid wash clothes that are still hanging in his closet. Even though they're not dirty, they wash them anyways because there may be dust mites on them after not being worn for a week or so.

As for Father, he is always stiff. He has never been able to show his feelings to anyone. Sometimes Thom wonders if he even has any emotions.

Considering that there are people in the house at all times, Thom can understand why his father could never ease up and relax like most other fathers would. Nevertheless, Thom admires him a great deal, always has and always will. Just like he will always love his Mother no matter how distant she may be physically; he knows he will protect her with his life.

As Thom continues to flip through the pages, another entry catches his eye.

*

September 10, 2079

Well, isn't this a pleasant surprise! Victor invited us over to his house today for afternoon tea. Can you imagine? Afternoon tea? We haven't had one of those, well, ever! He is such a gentleman. I wonder what we should bring. A bottle of wine just sounds wrong when you are invited to tea.

He didn't say why he wants to meet us, but I am hoping that he simply wants to know us better, just like we want to know him. Well, silly me. It's a Sunday. Why would he need a reason to invite someone over for tea?

*

That's interesting. Father never invited people over to the house socially. Every time he saw anyone entering the home, they usually look as emotionless as his father and they would go straight to his private library and close the doors. It was usually business. Often, they looked gloomier leaving the house than when they arrived, which is saying a lot.

Thom cannot recall ever seeing the Sullivans come to their house. Perhaps, it was one of those days when he was away at camp. But, then again, it was September. School would have already started by then. On a Sunday, he would usually be home. If he was, he would have definitely remembered his best friend's parents coming for a visit. Why could he not remember?

Brushing it off, Thom continues his reading. This next entry was written about a month after.

*

October 8, 2079

Big news today. Victor wants us to join the Legion. He knows that I am not a big fan of fighting, so he made sure to offer us jobs as specialists, not as soldiers. Because of my background in politics, he asked me if I would be interested in becoming his intelligence officer. I am not sure why the Legion would want me to be the intelligence officer. I have never held that position before in my life! Doesn't he have a bunch of spies already on the payroll that would be better suited for this job? Why me?

I am not sure how to answer him. I don't want to be rude, but I am really not interested in joining the Legion or any other military group, for that matter. It just seems so violent even if I am not going to be in the front line. Besides, I cannot leave Max in someone else's care. Who is going to pick him up from soccer practice if not me?

Victor also asked Philip to head the Legion's engineering department. Unlike me, he seems to be quite excited about the prospect. He has been working as the head of the science department for our old University for some time now. Even though he likes his job, he is eager for a change. Victor has convinced him that he is the best man for the job.

But I am not so sure that is truly the case. Don't get me wrong. I have absolute faith in my husband. He is absolutely brilliant and he can do anything he puts his mind to, but he is a Chemist, not an Engineer. Just like the job that Victor is offering me, the position is interesting, but he is hardly an expert in that field. While the two subjects may be related, they are very different in practice.

Then again, Philip is beside himself. In this new job, he will be responsible for ten times the number of employees and the salary is nearly triple of what the University is paying him. Yes, from a logical point of view, it is a good move, but I just don't know. We don't really need the money and he knows how I feel about the Legion, but I will not stop him if he wants to be a part of it.

The sad thing is, I think Victor can tell how much I hesitated. Instead of pushing either one of us to accept, he has given us two weeks to think it over.

*

Thom is very surprised to have read this entry. He had no idea that his father wanted to recruit the Sullivans. Knowing what he knows now, Thom is very curious as to why the highest ranking official in the Legion is so interested in the Sullivans. Even though Max's parents are both highly intelligent, he cannot think of anything else that would make them both so extraordinary that his father would invite them into his own home.

And, like Mrs. Sullivan wrote, his father was recruiting her for a position that's highly sensitive. Yet, she does not have the necessary experience for it. So, why? What does Father know about them that makes them so valuable?

To add icing to the cake, he even gave them two weeks to decide. The father that Thom knows would have given them probably ten minutes to discuss the terms and expected an acceptance thereafter. Otherwise, he would withdraw the offer immediately because as far as he is concerned, only an idiot would reject him, no matter what he is proposing.

So, it is clear to Thom that Max's parents are very important. Do they have connections that he is not aware of? Or, perhaps the more important question is, do they have connections that even *they* are not aware of? Because the Sullivans are so friendly, they know a great deal of people. Is it possible that they have associates who may be working for the Desiderios?

At the same time, because they know so many people in so many places, they can easily plead ignorance if they ever get caught on suspicion of collaborating with the rebels. It would be so easy for them to just say that they are visiting friends even if they're on a mission.

Thom cannot wait to see what happens next.

*

It's been ten days since Victor put the offer on the table. Philip is going to accept the job. He is really excited about it and wants me to accept mine, too. He likes to be able to come by during his breaks to just say "Hi" once in a while. He also would like to eat lunch together every day. He is such a sweet man. Just wait until he gets bored of eating lunch with his old lady every single day and wishes that he is hanging out with the guys once in a while!

OK, now to a more serious topic. After I voiced my concern about Max's after school care, Amelia has graciously offered to pick him up from school so the two boys can spend a few hours together. She promises that she will take very good care of him and that they will do their homework first before playing. She also mentioned that she has hired one of the best governesses, who's been helping her take care of Thom since he was born. So, Max should be in good hands.

I know Max would like that very much, but I am not sure if I can let go. After all, he is only six years old – practically a baby! I just took the training wheels off of his bicycle. I am not sure I am ready to take the training wheels off of him yet. What if he hurts himself? Sooner or later, though, I am going to have to let him go a little. He has to grow up sometime. I just hoped it would be later rather than sooner.

*

"Oh, yeah, I remember that!" Thom reminisces. "I guess Mrs. Sullivan did fold and accept the job after all."

Thom was very excited when his Mother told him that Max would be coming over to spend the afternoons with him. Those were such fun days! Old Mrs. Taylor was always trying to catch them doing something they were not supposed to, but with the two of them, they were able to outsmart her every time. It was the best! If it wasn't for

Max, Thom's childhood would have consisted of lots of expensive gadgets and nothing else. While some other children may envy the material things that he had, he certainly missed the love and attention that they got.

Here is another entry about Thom.

*

November 8, 2079

Before Amelia starts to pick Max up from school, we took him to the Richardsons' home so we can introduce him to everyone in the household. From what I hear, there are quite a few. And, it would be incredibly impolite for him to wander into rooms that he is not supposed to.

The strange thing is, just like the last time that we visited, Thom was not there again. Today is a Wednesday. Where in the world would he be on a school day? I'm a little concerned about Max staying here after school if the boy who lives here isn't even there.

*

There it is again. Thom doesn't remember when Max came to visit the house for the first time. Come on, why wouldn't he want to see his best friend?

It is starting to bother Thom that he doesn't remember events like this. He couldn't have been in football practice because he was only six and he didn't start playing sports until Junior High. He didn't have any other friends who he would visit and there was no other reason for him to be away from the house.

If he was at home, why does he not remember? Was he confined in a room during the time of the visits? Did his parents purposely prevent him from seeing them conduct business of any kind, even if it had to do with his best friend? What is the need for such secrecy, especially to a child? Thom's thoughts are getting more troubled by the minute.

Chapter 7: The Clues

Nevertheless, Thom realizes that he has spent way too much time going down memory lane. Even though it made for interesting reading, none of it has gotten him any closer to finding anyone. He needs to start getting more serious.

Now that Thom has finished reading the lovey dovey section of the Sullivans' lives, he is expecting the next section to be about their work. After all, if the entire notebook is about personal feelings, there is really no need to hide it under the floor board, is there? This next entry seems promising. It tells of the Sullivans' first day of work at the Legion.

*

December 1, 2079

It's the first day of work for Philip and me. Because we work in different divisions, we were separated almost as soon as we walked in the door. This place is huge! All of the hallways and the offices look so much the same. I am getting quite confused as to where I have been, but it's really exciting! Well, the orientation part is, anyways. I haven't actually started to do the real work yet since it's the first day.

There are so many people everywhere, but strangely, they all look so similar. Every one of them is wearing the same uniforms and has similar haircuts. Women have their hair in tight and severe looking buns and men have their hair buzzed off. It's a little weird. It's almost as if I am looking at clones. I haven't seen Victor though and I am not sure if I will. Being the head of this outfit, he is probably very busy and will not be able to meet with just any employee like myself.

Lieutenant Paul Gillnet is the one who took me around and introduced me to everyone. He is my immediate supervisor and I am to take orders directly from him and no one else. He is a very serious man. I don't think I heard him laugh even once at anything. And, I thought I was being quite humorous today. Oh, well, tough audience. Then again, very few people were in the laughing mood over there. It seems that most people are almost as stiff as Victor is.

I guess, in a way, he being the leader of the Legion has set the mood for all of the employees over there. I hope I don't have to be as somber as they are. It would really take the fun out of everything! I know, maybe Philip and I can be known as Mr. and Mrs. Nonconformance! That would be hilarious!

I don't know how Philip's first day of work went. I asked him, but all he said was it was good. Then, he tells me that he had to sign some confidentiality agreement and that he could not tell anyone about anything, even his own wife who worked in the same place. Go figure. He is a stickler to rules. I am sure I am not missing anything anyways.

*

So, it appears Gillnet should know Sonya Sullivan quite well. Now the question is, if he knows her, how well does he know Max? Knowing Mrs. Sullivan the way that he does, Thom is sure that she shared lots of stories and pictures of her precious boy with her boss. Under these circumstances, it would be nearly impossible for Gillnet not to know Max.

Yet, he is certainly playing dumb about him. Thom hasn't heard Gillnet talk about Max in any shape or form since he brought him in.

Wonder what does he know? Or, what does he not want Thom to know?

Flipping through the next few pages, there are several entries detailing Mrs. Sullivan's day at work. They all seem quite monotonous. She always goes to work at exactly 8AM and leaves at 5PM. She takes lunch at noon with her husband at the on-site cafeteria. According to her journal, her work seems to consist of reviewing documents and videos. Because her job also involves confidentiality, she has not written anything in there about the missions.

One thing that he does notice is that with each entry, her mood seems to be shifting. Also, the entries are further apart now. Instead of once every week or so, it is now once a month. Instead of the happy jolly golly entries seen in the beginning, the writing has become dry and to the point, like this one.

*

August 19, 2080

Work is getting very hectic. There is a great deal of information coming in for us to review and I am seeing disturbing signs in the world. I am worried about the state of this dominion. Philip is, too.

*

The Sullivans had only worked for the Legion for close to nine months and they already seemed distressed. What is the information that Mrs. Sullivan was reviewing? And, as the head of Engineering, what was Philip researching that gave him reservations?

Then, curiously, the entries stop for the rest of the year. There is no mention of work and not even an occasional update on how Max is doing. He would have just started first grade by that time. Being a proud mother, she surely would have something to say about his new teacher or classroom. But, no, there is no mention of it at all, which can only mean one thing. She was preoccupied with something bigger that was very troubling.

The next entry does not start until nearly a year later.

*

April 20, 2081

Well, at least I figured out part of the reason why Victor wanted me to be his intelligence officer. There is just so much information coming into this office, and more than half of them are rumors and hearsays that are just plain wrong. Some of them may even be detrimental if we acted upon them, causing thousands of deaths, if not more.

Unfortunately, most of the team members seem to want to jump at anything sensational, thinking or hoping that it would give them a big promotion, not realizing or even caring about the possible consequences. The others who are less motivated just sit on their information and don't do anything with it.

I guess Victor needed a fresh pair of eyes that are completely unbiased to make intelligent decisions on which ones may be valid. I am so glad that I convinced him not to act on one this morning. I dread to think of what would have happened if we did.

*

Good point. The Legion does seem a little uptight at times, well, maybe all the time. But, if Mrs. Sullivan thinks that is the reason his father went out of his way to recruit her, she is much more naïve than Thom had originally thought. If that were the only reason, he could have easily gotten his assistant to find any intelligent person just coming out of the University for the job.

Flipping ahead a few pages, Thom comes across a lighter entry. He is glad to see that the old good natured Mrs. Sullivan is back, at least temporarily, to write on a subject that is of a more personal nature.

*

March 6, 2082

We had a wonderful visitor today. It's my dear old sister Lillian! I haven't seen her in ages. She looks absolutely radiant. I think she is with child, but she is mums about it. I am not going to ask just in case she isn't. But, she has been touching her tummy a lot and she looks SO happy! I hope she is. She would make a great mother.

I remember when I was expecting Max. How can I possibly not? I was always happy, even when I should be in a foul mood. Nothing could get me down! Philip was very happy, too, since he could get away with just about anything!

It is an absolutely wonderful feeling having a life grow inside of you.

Of course, life on the road may be hard for an expectant mother and an infant, but that's her way of life. I personally wouldn't want to choose it, but she likes it. Ever since she married Adam three years ago, they've been traveling with his family.

*

It's nice to hear about Mrs. Sullivan's family. Thom knows so little about them. Max has never really spoken about any of them. He is not sure how many there are or where they are.

All he knows is that he has a great deal of extended family, but not a single one lives in the dominion. He has seen photographs of them, but can't really keep track since he only met them on rare occasions.

It's almost like Thom's family. That's probably one reason why they are such great friends because they are both an only child and neither one of them grew up with their cousins. So, they eventually came to see each other as family.

It's an interesting family that this Lillian has, though. Wonder why they are always traveling?

*

March 30, 2082

Lillian and Adam are back. As I expected, she is with child, but she has been having a very difficult time with her pregnancy. She has been very ill and the traveling is really putting a toll on her health. So, they will be staying with us until their child is born.

Even though she doesn't admit it, I can tell that she is not happy about it, but Adam has convinced her that it's for the best. They don't really have a choice. They don't want to risk losing the baby or her, for that matter. There is no telling what complications she may have if she doesn't rest.

Of course, not to look like an ungrateful guest, Lillian insists that if she were to stay with anyone in the world, it would be with us. What a silly goose! The truth of the matter is I am overjoyed to have them stay with us. It's been a long time since we had other members of the family stay for a while. They usually come to visit for a few hours and leave.

Even Max's grandparents have not stayed for long. The last time they did was when my mother stayed for two weeks when Max was born. Since then, we hardly have seen her or grandpa. We don't know when we will see any of them again.

Lillian's visit will definitely give us a break from work – that's for sure! We definitely need a distraction. Besides, Max gets to know another member of the family better, which is a rare treat.

*

Thom vaguely remembers an Aunt Lillian and Uncle Adam, but nothing much. Max just told him that he had relatives staying at his house for a while, but he doesn't remember him mentioning anything else.

*

June 26, 2082

I am so glad that I convinced Victor not to act on some of the information that we received at headquarters. I am so amused at the amount of misinformation coming through. I am beginning to wonder if someone is intentionally feeding us false information so we miss the real important ones. Then again, these lies are not innocent ones, either. Perhaps, there is more than one suspect in play?

*

Interesting, what else is happening now? Who was she insinuating? Is Mrs. Sullivan trying to say that there is a mole or two within the Legion?

*

November 3, 2082

What a joyous day! Little Sean was born. He is a tiny one, like Max. He only weighs 6 pounds 2 ounces and is 19 inches long. He is such a sweet little thing! He hardly cries at all. He only fusses when he is hungry or needs a diaper change. Otherwise, he is either sleeping or staring at his surroundings with awe.

Max is not sure what to make of him, though. I can see a lot of confusion on his face when the baby cries. He just stands there and looks for his Aunt Lillian. He has no idea what to do with a baby.

I don't blame him, though. He has never been around one before. So, I guess in a way, this is a good little practice for him. That way when he does have a child of his own, he won't be so shocked. Let's hope he doesn't immediately call for his wife when his child cries. After all, Philip is a great father. I hope he takes after him.

He doesn't know why, but Thom chuckles when he reads about his friend's childhood dilemma. Perhaps, it's because he can relate. If he had to watch a baby when he was nine years old, he probably wouldn't know what to do, either.

*

December 15, 2082

Well, Lillian, Adam, and Sean are leaving us today. That's too bad. I have grown quite fond of them. They are to join the rest of their family in the outskirts of town. I am going to miss them greatly! We have shared so many stories.

Some are fun, like the story of how she and Adam met. That one is a doozy! I cannot believe they actually got married after that little charade. I promised Lillian that I won't tell anyone. So, I won't even write it down. Suffice it to say, it's one for the record books.

Then again, there are some troubling tales, too. Her family has seen some horrible things. Towns have been burned down and people have been killed all over the place. It seems we live in harsh times, but those living within the dominion are oblivious of any of that. We haven't heard any of those things.

The Legion makes sure that we are sheltered from such horrible news. Is it better to be happy and ignorant or to be sad and knowledgeable? In either case, since the Legion is intent on keeping everyone in the dark, I am going to keep it quiet, too, at least for a little while.

*

That is a very good question. Thom isn't sure which he would pick, either. Since his father is the leader of the Legion, he probably would pick the former just because he knows that's what his father would have wanted him to do. But, a part of him is questioning exactly what kind of horrific news Mrs. Sullivan referring to. In either case, it sounds like his father is controlling the media, only letting out news that he wants others to know, which is troubling even to Thom.

Back in December 2082, the war had not started yet. In fact, it wouldn't start for another three years. Looking at history, though, wars don't happen overnight.

There is usually some compelling reason that's been brewing for a while before the actual fighting begins. Is the information that Mrs. Sullivan is writing about the impetus that started the war? If so, this information can actually lead him to the Desiderios. If Max is working for the rebellion, it would also lead him to Max.

Looking at the clock, Thom realizes that he needs to stop reading for the day. If he hangs around his room any longer, the rest of the Legion will become suspicious and come snooping. Better to keep all three journals with him at all times to make sure that no one else reads this. He needs to put on his "General" face and go to his weekly standing meeting with the other officers.

*

"Good morning, everyone. I trust you all had a good night's sleep," Thom starts the meeting with an upbeat tone.

"Why are you so jolly this morning?" Lieutenant Gillnet replies with a suspicious look on his face.

"Why? Is it a crime to try to be cheerful at these meetings now?"

"Whatever," Gillnet mutters under his breath.

"What? I didn't catch you." Thom replies, knowing full well what he said.

"Nothing, sir. Have you heard any word from your friend Max?"

"No," Thom replies in a more serious tone. He is interested in seeing what everyone else is thinking right now. With a question like that, it must pique someone's interest. "What about the rest of you?" He continues as he looks in everyone's eyes.

"No, sir," Lieutenant Marcel replies while the others shake their heads or shrug their shoulders.

"What have you guys done to try to locate him?"

"I didn't realize this has become top priority," Major Fouke remarks with a slight jest.

"Excuse me? Do I hear dissension amongst the ranks? I thought I made it perfectly clear that we must locate him. With his skills and knowledge, if he falls into the enemy's hand, he could be used against us. Do I need to remind you that he knows every one of you and our location?"

"Sorry, sir," General Hawk responds emotionlessly. "You are right. We must retrieve him. I have dispatched ten men for the search team and have expanded our search to a twenty miles radius from the dominion, but still no sign of him."

Hm, Hawk's first name is John. Thom studies his right hand man and wonders if Mrs. Sullivan was running off to meet with him on the day she disappeared. He looks for anything that might give him away, but he doesn't see even the slightest tick. If anyone has a poker face, it's General Hawk.

"Thank you, Hawk. That's much better." Then, turning towards Mrs. Sullivan's former employer, he nods and says, "What about you, Gillnet? What have you found?"

"Nothing, sir."

"Where have you and your men looked?"

"We have been concentrating in the battlefield area to look for clues."

"And?"

"We traced the enemy to the river, but lost track of them after that."

Either his men are completely incompetent or they are pretending to be because they have no intention of finding Max. After all, even though none of them said anything when he introduced Max to them, he knows that none of them cared for Max because of his low rank.

Changing the topic, he says, "Do we have any more news about the Desiderios or El Diablo, credible ones anyways? I don't want to hear anymore chitchats or gossips like I normally do," Thom says as he rolls his eyes.

No one says anything.

"You guys are as useful as an umbrella on a sunny day. I expect somebody to find something useful next time we meet. Meeting dismissed," Thom says as he waves for everyone to leave.

Even though he sounds irritated, he is actually glad that they have nothing to say. Now, he can go back to his reading in peace.

*

February 15, 2083

Paul has given me a strange assignment today. Instead of reviewing information, he wants me to chat with all of the high ranking officers and get to know them better. Strange. I didn't think he was the kind who wants to be sociable.

He didn't tell me why, but I didn't ask because I know he won't tell me anyways. Since yesterday was Valentine's Day, maybe he feels like being loving for once and wants me to chat and relax. On second thought, nah, not him.

*

Well, she is right. Gillnet has never been the loving kind. Thom has never seen him have a friendly conversation with anyone nor has he ever mentioned any member of his family. No one even knows if he is married or not. He does not wear a wedding ring, but that doesn't say much.

Almost nobody wears one in the Legion. It's protocol, actually. If any of them ever get caught, they don't want to let their enemies know that they have loved ones at home that they can kidnap or hurt in order to get information out of them.

In any case, Gillnet must be trying to spy on the other officers. If he is, he must be suspecting someone. The question is who?

*

March 11, 2083

It's amazing how uptight everyone is at work! No matter how hard I try, I cannot get any of the officers to relax and chat with me. I even offered them muffins and cupcakes to try to bribe them into being more sociable. They gladly ate the goodies, which probably means that I am a pretty good little baker if I do so say myself, but most of the conversations consist of short and dry answers.

Take Lieutenant Marcel, for example, when I asked him if he is married. His answer was simply "yes." It wasn't until I followed it up with more probing questions did he offer any further details. When I asked, though, he did give seemingly truthful answers. If he didn't want me to know about his family business, he could have simply lied and said he wasn't married, which would have ended the entire conversation. So, I guess that's something. I just have to be VERY specific with the questions or I'll get a very generic answer or one that does not answer the intended question.

And then, there were a few that were completely useless. When I asked Major Fouke whether or not he was married, he answered with another question and said, "Why do you want to know?" When I said, "I would like to know you better." His response was "Why do you want to know me better?" It only got worse after that. There was really no point.

*

So, Marcel is married. After having known him for five years, Thom never knew that before. Perhaps, it's his fault for not asking, but in either case, it's good to know that Mrs. Sullivan finds him to be truthful.

Thom ponders if he should go and ask him some well-planned questions to see if he knows something about Max's whereabouts. He had said he didn't know anything about Max, but perhaps he asked the wrong questions.

What exactly did Thom ask during the meeting? Thinking back, he realizes that the question "What about the rest of you?" was *way* too generic for someone like Marcel.

As for Fouke, Thom knew that he would not have cooperated anyways. He almost never does. It's amazing that he rose to the rank of Major. He must be very good at what he does because his sly remarks can sometimes be construed as insubordination. Just about every word that comes out of his mouth is sarcasm.

Maybe he's mad at the world or something.

*

June 9, 2083

Philip and I are taking a break from work while Max is having a sleepover at Thom's house. We are going mountain climbing today. Even though dear hubby is worried that I might hurt or even kill myself from falling down a cliff or something, I assured him that I will be VERY careful. In fact, I am going to tie myself to him. So, if I fall, he better catch me or we can die together. While that may sound romantic, it's not something I plan on doing until we are both very old and possibly toothless.

*

After reading this entry, Thom remembers that day when Max slept over. But, as he recalls, it was more than one day. He stayed for almost two weeks straight. It was great fun, though! The only one who put a damper on it was Mrs. Taylor. Even though it was during summer vacation, she still insisted that they learn something.

It seems that she couldn't grasp the concept of what a summer vacation is. Oh, well, studying with Max was a lot more fun than doing it alone.

Wonder what Mr. and Mrs. Sullivan did for two weeks in the mountains? Did they discover anything? Since Mrs. Sullivan usually likes to write down light hearted events about her family, she would have written something about their adventure.

As Thom looks through the next page, he realizes that there is nothing in there about their trip whatsoever, which is very odd indeed. Whatever it is that they did, they did not want to leave a trail. Perhaps they saw something they shouldn't. Or, they met someone they don't want anyone to know about.

There is absolutely nothing written over the next six months. Thom is particularly interested in the missing period. Being an intelligence officer, Mrs. Sullivan obviously knows when to keep quiet and when she should make the announcement so the world can hear. Then, the next entry appears.

*

January 5, 2084

Philip and I are resigning from our positions today. It's just too much for us and we cannot go on working there knowing what we know.

*

That's a very short entry. After working for a little over four years, the Sullivans have resigned under what looks to be a superficial, albeit suspicious excuse. What is it that they know that would lead them to quit their very lucrative jobs? All that Thom has read so far are just hints, but nothing he can truly go on.

There have been mentions of misinformation that led to disasters. There have been mysteriously undocumented trips. And, there have been uncomfortably long periods of total silence.

He rubs his temples in frustration. Thom has to sleep on it.

Now, where would be a good place for him to hide these journals? Looking around his room, he realizes that there is nowhere safe from prying eyes. Places like under the bed or in the closet are dead giveaways.

Then, he decides that the best place is in plain sight. He takes a slipcover off of three different books about the same width as the journals and places them over them. Then, he puts them in three separate shelves before turning himself in for the night.

Chapter 8: Round Two

"Hey, Max, how are you feeling today?" Violet asks after bursting into his room.

Trying to get a clear view of the woman who rudely interrupted his slumber, Max squints and blinks several times through blurry eyes. "Hey, Violet, what time is it?"

"Your favorite time of the day!"

"Oh, no. Are we doing that again today?"

"What? You think just because you had a rough day yesterday that I will let you sleep in today? Not a chance!"

Violet reaches over and drags him out of bed.

"Where is our fearless leader this morning? You couldn't convince him to get up today?" Max asks as he yawns again.

"Did I hear that right? Did you just call Trip *our fearless leader*? This is a good sign!" Violet says excitedly.

"Huh? What are you talking about?"

Violet is glad to hear that Max is so comfortable with the rebels that he is officially recognizing Trip as his leader. To top it off, he said it so casually that he didn't even realize what he had said.

She giggles as she pushes him through the door.

Just like the previous day, she shoots him multiple times and enjoys every moment of it. While he has not been able to dodge any of her attacks completely, Violet is pleased to see that he has already improved significantly since yesterday. Nobody has shown as much promise as Max has.

"So, how do you feel?" Violet asks.

"Still sore." Max answers truthfully.

"That's to be expected, but do you feel more like a *warrior* now?" she says with tongue in cheek.

"Not even close."

"Oh, you are just being modest. Come on, let's fill that tummy of yours back up, shall we?" Violet says as she pats Max's stomach lightly.

After devouring his breakfast like the day before, Violet takes Max to Trip's garden and says, "Are you ready to resume our conversation?"

Looking puzzled, Max replies, "Sure, but I thought we finished our discussion. What else is there that you want to talk to me about?"

"How much do you know about your friend Thom?"

At the sound of his best friend's name, Max's gut instinctively wants to spill out all of the childhood escapades that they have had and all of the mischievous things that they got away with, but he knows that's not what Violet wants to know. Max is not sure which direction she is going, but decides to let her drive it and see what she really wants to hear.

"I thought I knew quite a bit, but I am not really sure now."

"Okay, for starters, can you trust him?"

"Yes, with my life, at least I think I can."

"Well, that doesn't sound like you are all that sure after all. Why have you changed your mind?"

"I haven't really. It's not that I don't trust him as a person. It's that I don't know if I can trust him not to accidentally disclose things to those around him. I definitely do not trust any of the goons in the Legion headquarters, and he's surrounded by them."

"Is there a particular one that you are most suspicious of?"

Thinking for a second, they all look shady to him. "No, they all look the same. None of them were particularly friendly when we first met."

"Do you remember whom you met?"

Going back to their first meeting, Max's face starts to turn white. He just realized that General Hawk, the one who his mother was supposed to meet is in that group. Violet can tell from his expression that he has made the connection.

Looking at Violet with anger in his eyes, he asks in as calm of a voice as he can, "Are you suggesting that one of them murdered my parents?"

"Yes, if not them directly, it was definitely someone connected to one of them."

"What are we waiting for? Let's get them!"

"Hold on, let's not get too hasty. Even though we know where their headquarters are, it's suicide to try to storm it. Besides, there is one more person who we are trying to get, who is much bigger than any of them."

Max tilts his head in confusion. "You don't mean Thom, do you? I really don't think he would have anything to do with my parents' death. He loves them almost as much as I do."

"Oh, I don't doubt that. Like you, I think we can trust him, too, but it's someone related to him."

"Who?"

"Do you honestly not know who his father is?"

Looking even more puzzled, he asks, "Mr. Richardson?"

"Wow, you really don't know, do you? Considering that you call him by that name, it's pretty obvious that you don't know that he is the one pulling all of the strings in the Legion."

"Why would he? Just because Thom is the General doesn't make his father anything."

"Wow, I thought you were smart. I will give you a moment to think it over."

Before he could get offended by her sly remark, a light bulb turns on in his head.

"No! It's just the opposite. Thom is the General *because* his father is the head of the Legion! That explains why his father was never there when I visited. It's not that he was out of town like we thought. It's that he was across town calling the shots!"

"Bravo! I think he's got it! Don't worry, you're not *that* slow. Thom didn't know either until recently."

"Why would his father keep his position a secret from his own son?"

"Ironically, Victor stayed away from home all those years *because* he wanted his son to have a normal childhood. If he had told him what he really did for a living, the other children may have been afraid to play with him in fear of his father's wrath."

"What wrath? I was his closest friend. What kind of wrath did he bestow on me?" Then, his face turns ashen again, "Is that why my parents were killed?!"

"Oh, no, silly! Victor didn't have your parents killed because of your friendship with his son. That would be completely idiotic!" Violet says as she tries to reassure Max, who is now completely shaken by this conversation.

Of course, she chooses her words carefully. She didn't say that Victor did not kill Max's parents, simply that if he did, it was not because of the friendship. She is not sure if he got that. "Do you need a minute?"

Taking a deep breath, Max says, "No, no, I am good. I want to know. Please continue."

"In a way, Victor thinks he is being a good father, but at the same time, he is also very power hungry. More than once, his greed has won over his heart."

"So, you are saying that despite wanting to protect Thom, Victor has been using his son, so he can gain more control."

"Well said."

After a short pause, Max looks at Violet suspiciously, "So, why are you telling me this?"

Smiling, Violet says, "Patience, I cannot tell you that yet."

"Why not?"

"You are not ready. You need more training."

"What am I training for?"

"A special mission that requires you to be at the top of your game."

"Why me?"

"Isn't it obvious?"

"Humor me."

"Look, Max. I am not trying to be difficult. It's just that I really cannot tell you yet. When Trip and I think you are ready, we will give you all of the details that your heart desires. But, before then, it would be irresponsible for me to tell you anymore."

"You are such a tease!" Max grunts.

*

After reading about the mountains, Thom *has* to investigate. It's obvious that the Sullivans found something there and he just has to find out what. Besides, there have been numerous reported sightings of El Diablo around the mountain ridge. This just cannot be a coincidence. His gut tells him that something went on in these mountains that prompted the Sullivans to resign. And, that this something has everything to do with the infamous Devil of the rebels.

After telling his men that he is going on a secret mission, he leaves General Hawk in charge.

Changing into civilian outfit and leaving all traces of the military behind, he packs his climbing gear, canteen, food, and the journals before heading south towards the mountains.

His nerves are on edge because he has never climbed a real mountain on his own before. He has no idea what he may encounter.

Knowing that the Sullivans climbed it, however, Thom is confident that he can do it, too. After all, the military has trained him well. In addition to the simulation rock climbing lessons, the survival skills that he learned in his basic training should prepare him for such a task. At least, that is what he is hoping.

He hops in the back of a truck that's heading south with a couple of other kids, undoubtedly just regular teenagers on a camping trip. The truck reaches the first mountain pass and drops Thom off, with the kids waving at him as they drive away. He waves back and starts the trek up the large mountain.

*

After hours of climbing, he stops to take in the view. He is high enough to see many things from afar. He cannot

124

believe how beautiful it is. As he admires the view, however, he is becoming more and more convinced that the Desiderios are hiding in the mountains somewhere. He can see everything from here, including the dominion from a bird's eye view. He can even make out where the Legion headquarters are from where he is standing.

Yet, he is frustrated that he has not found a single trace of the rebellion or the Sullivans. There is nothing but nature here – no trash, no remnants of old campsites, and no signs of long-dead fires. The only things he sees are sporadic patches of flattened grass that have been trampled. Since travelers and hikers have been known to come to the mountains on occasion, these could have been created by anyone.

Overhead, there are the occasional eagles flying. He even sees some goats scaling the mountains not far from him. The breeze brings out such fresh and crisp air that he cannot help but take a moment to take it all in.

"Well, now is as good of a time as any to take a break!" He says to himself as he sits down and takes a bite to eat. Then, he takes out the journal again. But, instead of Max's or Sonya's, he decides to take a look at Philip's. Even though inside are mostly engineering designs that do not interest him, he wants to peruse through it anyways. He is hoping that Philip has left some clues that may come in handy.

*

The first entry in Philip's journal starts on the first day of work at the Legion headquarters. It contains basically a laundry list of items. The first line is the name and contact information of his supervisor, Lieutenant Marcel.

"Wow, small world." Thom is starting to wonder why both supervisors were under his direct command.

This cannot be a coincidence, can it?

But then again, all of the division heads report to him. Maybe, he is reading too much into this.

Back to the journal, Thom glances through the rest of the first page. It contains fifteen names of other engineers in the group, none of which he recognizes, which is to be expected. On occasion, he gets to mingle with the soldiers, but, as the General, Thom hardly gets the chance to meet the other workers within the departments. He has no reason to.

Then, Thom flips through several pages of chemical formulas that he knows nothing about. Philip usually writes a short sentence or two underneath each formula. Even thought they were written in English, it might as well have been written in Greek as far as he is concerned. None of it makes any sense to him.

He was never any good in Chemistry or Physics, or any of the sciences, for that matter. He studied just enough to pass the courses and forgot everything he learned soon after the final exams. Academics were never his strong suit.

He has always preferred sports, which probably explains why he is one of the toughest men in the Legion. In a way, Max and he complement one another perfectly.

As he flips through the pages, the formulas seem to get more complicated with each page. The writing is also getting more hurried. Some of the sentences are starting to look like a bunch of scribbling. But, Thom notices there are some words that are clearly written, like *devastation*, *annihilation*, *massive*, and *explosion*.

It's pretty clear that whatever Philip was working on was a weapon, a big one at that. It is also evident that whatever he was working on was eating him alive.

Thom quickly flips to the last entry. It is dated on the day that the Sullivans resigned. From the looks of it, the formula is not finished. There is nothing written beneath it to annotate it. Did Mr. Sullivan quit his job so he didn't have to finish creating whatever it was that he was supposed to make?

On the last page, there are also two words that are plainly visible, *Algoma* and *Kerbasy*. Where has he heard those words from before? Are they names of a person or a place? For the life of him, he cannot remember, but whatever they are, they must be important.

Thom closes the journal to rest his eyes. He's far too tired to do anything more.

*

An hour later, he wakes up and continues on his excursion up the mountain. After five grueling more hours climbing, Thom comes to a stop underneath an overhanging on the side of the mountain. After checking for predators who might call this place home, he decides to rest.

Sitting down, he lets out a loud sigh. Nothing! He has found absolutely no sign of anything useful.

At least in the Sullivans' estate, he found these journals. Having spent twice as much time on this mountain, he has nothing to show for. He decides to pitch his tent here for the night. He will sleep on it and see if his luck changes for the better in the morning.

As he gets ready to hammer a stake into the ground, he notices that there is a small square hole on the ground about 15 feet from where he is.

Excited that he might have caught a possible scent of the trail, he looks around to see if he can see any clues as to whether or not the Sullivans stayed here. If they did, he is at least on the right track. Of course, this tent could have been pitched by hundreds of other hikers who may have traveled this way, but this is more than he has gotten all day.

After looking at the area a little more, he sees three other identical holes that look like they were made when someone pitched a tent about 10 feet by 10 feet in size. Studying the holes more closely, it looks as if the erosion of the terrain has covered much of them back up. Over time, the square holes became square indentations, which means the dirt may have also covered up some other potential clues.

Since it has been eight years since the Sullivans' trip, he tries to dig a little deeper underneath the square area of the tent to see if there is anything of value that has since been buried.

Another hour goes by, and all he has found are rocks and branches, nothing more. Giving up for the night, he finally sets up a tent and gets some shut eye.

*

Poke, poke. "Huh, what in the world?" Thom is jerked awake by someone or something nudging him. As he opens his eyes slowly, he feels something hit him hard and the rest is blank.

*

"Look who we have here." Thom hears a man's voice speak.

His head throbs intensely as he tries to see who's talking. Then, he realizes that he has a blindfold on and his hands and feet are tied behind his back.

Crap! He's been captured! Thom's heart begins to beat even faster than before as he begins to hyperventilate a little.

"What's the matter? Never been a captive before?" the voice says sarcastically.

"Who are you and what do you want?"

"Hey, you don't get to ask the questions. We do." The same man says as he kicks his shin just hard enough to create a bruise later on.

"Ouch!" Thom says instinctively.

"Oh, you big baby. That doesn't hurt! I could have hit you much harder."

"OK, let's get down to business," a woman's voice says.

"Who are you?" Thom asks as he looks in the direction of the second voice.

"Never mind that. Where did you get these journals?"

Oh, Crap! He never once thought that he was going to be captured. Now, they have the Sullivans' journals. "They are mine." Thom replies.

"Liar," the man says as he kicks him in the same spot.

"Ouch, stop that!" Thom exclaims as the man snickers.

"Since you are going to play dumb, I guess we have to take it up a notch. Get ready to cut off his pinky," the woman says.

"Hold on a second! That's a little harsh, don't you think? So what if I took those journals? Are you going to cut off every man's finger just because he took them?" Thom protests.

"No, but we don't have a problem cutting off fingers if you keep lying to us," the man replies.

Pretending to be a petty thief who just happens to be nosy, he says, "OK, OK, I found them when I went through the owner's house. I am sorry! I promise to give them back. Now, there, are you happy?"

"Not good enough," the woman says as the man grabs hold onto his pinky. Thom can feel the cold metal of a blade resting on his skin.

Taking a deep breath, Thom realizes that he needs to get serious. He has no idea who these people are. For all he knows, they'll kill him even if he tells them everything.

"Can you at least take my blindfold off so I can see who I am talking to?" Thom asks.

Even though he is pretty sure they are not going to honor his request, he has to try so he can buy some time. One thing he did learn from the Legion is how to tie a mean knot and how to untie one. Judging from the voices, they are both in front of him. He is trying desperately to loosen his hands as quietly as he can, hoping that nobody catches him before he succeeds.

"Don't bother, that knot is foolproof. I did it myself," the woman says.

Shoot, they can see him. What to do? What to do? The gears in his mind are turning as he tries to figure out a plan to escape.

Then, the man says, "As to your question, I am sure you already know the answer is no. Why should we let you see who we are? So, you can go back to your daddy and tell him about the big, bad people who kidnapped you so he can come back and burn us down?"

Having heard these words, Thom is a little curious. "So, I see you know who I am."

"Yes, Thomas Richardson. We know who you are and we know who your father is," the woman says dryly.

"So, why are you playing this game?" Thom says seriously.

"We are not playing. You are the one toying with us. I am going to ask you again, where did you get the journals?"

"I am not lying. I did find it in the owner's home and I do intend on putting it back after reading it."

"How do you know the owner?"

"They are friends of mine."

"You robbed a friend's house? What kind of person are you?"

"I didn't rob the house. I was looking for clues."

"Clues to what?"

"To their whereabouts."

As soon as he utters those words, a hand comes to the back of his head and the blindfold is off. Thom adjusts his eyes and sees that he is in a small standard interrogation room. All four walls are white, and there are no windows of any kind. The only light is from one solitary bulb on top of the ceiling. There is a mirror, likely a one-way one, across from where he is sitting. There are two wooden chairs across from the long wooden table in front of him. Both the man and the woman are wearing casual civilian clothes, and he has never seen them before.

"Since you know who I am, but I don't know you, I think I am at a disadvantage here. Who are you?" Thom asks.

"Take a guess," the woman says.

"I have no idea. Are you a member of the Legion?" Thom asks as he plays dumb.

"Oh, please. I thought we were past that."

"OK, so, are you a part of the rebellion?"

"Is that the only option here? You are either with one or the other?"

"I don't know. Are you?"

"No," the woman says after a short pause.

The uncomfortable second of silence gives the woman away, but Thom is not about to call her bluff yet. After thinking for a second, he replies, "Are you related to the Sullivans?"

"Ah, now you are getting warmer."

"Are you Lillian?" Thom asks curiously.

Pointing at her nose, she says, "Bing, bing, bing. Give the man a cigar. He finally got it."

"I assume that means you are Adam."

"Guilty as charged," Adam says as he tips his hat.

"How is baby Sean doing?"

"Ah, so you have been reading the journal quite thoroughly. Did you enjoy invading my sister's privacy?"

"Look, I understand that you are upset, but I sincerely want to find my friend Max and his parents and I am assuming you want the same. So, can you untie me now?"

"Absolutely not. Just because we are searching for the same people does not mean that we are on the same side. You are the General of the Legion. What makes you think I can trust you?"

"OK, I guess I have not given you a reason to trust me, but I trust that we both want the same thing. So, the best way to reach that is to work together."

"Blah, blah, blah. How trite. Any idiot could have said that."

"What do you want me to say?"

Lillian looks deep into his eyes and asks, "What did you do with Max?"

"I didn't do anything with him. He just vanished after the last battle. That is how I found the journals. I went to his parents' house hoping to find something that could help me figure it all out."

"That's not what I am talking about."

"Then, what?"

"When you dragged Max into the Legion, what kind of diabolical plans did you have for him?"

"I don't understand the question," Thom answers sincerely.

"Oh, come on. You know perfectly well that he cannot stand the Legion, but you enlisted him anyways. I am not even sure if that is legal. It's not like he was being drafted. So, why?"

"I don't really know where you are going with this, but I honestly thought I was doing him a favor. I know he never wanted to join, but I found out that he quit school and he didn't seem to have any gainful employment. With the war waging on, I figured joining the Legion was the best thing for him."

"So, what? Now, you are playing his father?"

"No, that's not what I'm trying to do."

"So, what are you trying to do?"

Thom knows that they are fishing for something with this line of questioning, but he is trying to figure out what is it that they are going after.

"OK, you want to know the truth? Fine, I will tell you the truth. I need a friend by my side. I have been in the Legion for five years now. Even though I have risen in rank, I have not found anyone I truly believe I can call a friend. I know that's very selfish of me, knowing that Max does not want to be part of this, but I need him with me."

Lillian cannot believe her ears. Here he is, the General of the Legion, admitting that he is still a child at heart and needs a friend. A part of her really feels for him, but the other part of her wants to be absolutely sure that he can be trusted before letting him in. She just has to figure out the question that she needs to ask to test him. What can she ask that will check to see that he is as pure as he pretends to be? Can it be true that this high ranking officer is truly is in the dark about everything that the Legion is doing?

"What is Victor planning now?"

"Nothing. He handed the reins over to me and I am now in charge of the entire Legion."

Lillian laughs as she hears how gullible Thom is. Thom just looks at her in confusion. Why is she laughing?

Lillian signals for Adam to come with her, and they leave the interrogation room before entering a second room, just as small as the previous one and dimly lit.

"So, what do you think?" Lillian asks her husband.

"I think we can trust him."

"Me, too," Lillian says as she nods her head. Then, turning towards Violet and Trip, she asks, "Do you concur?"

During this entire interrogation, El Diablo and the Warrior have been watching through the one-sided mirror from the second room. Trip nods his head and takes his leave.

Violet announces, "There you have it. He concurs. As do I. It seems Max has a true friend there. You know what to do."

With that, Violet takes her leave.

*

During the time that Lillian and Adam stayed with the Sullivans, they shared many stories with one another. Because of their sensitive nature, however, not one of them has ever made it into Sonya's journal. One of which is the burning of Algoma, Trip's homeland.

Being a member of the Kerbasy tribe, Adam and his family know Violet and her family very well. They have traveled with one another for many generations. Adam was there personally to witness the total destruction that the Legion left behind that fateful day when Trip became an orphan.

Adam was only eleven years old at the time, but he still remembers that day vividly. He has never seen so much death nor smelled so much burned flesh before or since that day. He made it his personal mission to take care of Trip as his younger brother on the day that he met him.

While Violet helped Trip learn how to be the best fighter he could be, Adam taught him some of the finer arts of life, like how to talk to girls and how to roast the best goose he has ever tasted.

While Trip learned all of these skills, he certainly never used them in real life, at least not in public for anyone to see. After all, Trip has never been on a date nor stepped foot in the kitchen.

Nevertheless, Adam prides himself in the fact that he took him in under his wing, at least for a little bit.

Lillian met Adam when they were both children – way back then before all of this misery started happening and the tribe still made their regular stops in Balavan. Whey Adam turned 18, he was granted permission to come into the dominion to be with Lillian with the promise that he would return with his new bride as soon as he could. Within the year, they became a wedded couple and rejoined the tribe to travel the world.

Unlike Violet, however, Adam and Lillian chose not to join the Desiderios formally.

That does not mean that they are not willing to lend a hand here and there. Hence, when Thom asked Lillian whether or not she is a member of the rebels and she answered negatively, she's technically telling the truth.

Since the war began, Lillian and her husband have been living in their secret hideout in the mountains, essentially acting as the scouts for the Desiderios. Whenever they see something or someone suspicious, they notify Trip.

Of course, Lillian would have never realized what a wonderful place the mountains were if it wasn't for Philip and Sonya. After their vacation, Sonya immediately realized what a strategic place it is. There are numerous paths and hidden passageways that zigzag through the mountains. She immediately began telling her sister where the best places are for a person to disappear if they needed to. She even hinted that it would be a great place for Trip to *set up shop* someday.

Before long, Lillian became curious and decided to take a break from the traveling to scope the place out for herself. Soon, Trip agreed that it would be the perfect location to place the headquarters for the Desiderios. Over the next two years, the Desiderios secretly lined up their defenses around the mountain before the war began against the Legion.

Chapter 9: The Reunion

Putting their poker faces back on, Lillian and Adam go back to the interrogation room.

As Adam begins to untie the knots on Thom's hands and feet, Lillian says, "Be careful what you are about to do. Even though we are freeing you, we will not be letting you go."

"What? Why not? That doesn't even make any sense."

"We cannot have you telling your daddy where you've been, now, can we?"

"But I don't know where you are."

"Oh, but you do. Or, would you like for me to knock you out again and dump you in the streets?" Adam asks sarcastically.

"Um, is that a serious option?" Thom replies with confusion.

"No," Lillian says as she rolls her eyes.

"So, I am to be your prisoner now?"

"Yes, kind of. You will be free to go as you please, with limits, of course. For example, you cannot leave the building and you cannot go into certain forbidden rooms."

"That's not free at all!"

"Are you complaining again? Would you rather be sitting in a jail cell, instead? Or, I can lock you in this room." Adam crosses his arms and stares at him with an exasperated expression.

"OK, OK, never mind. Sorry I asked."

Lillian and Adam exit the room, leaving him alone with the door open.

"Are they serious? They are just going to let me wander around here without an escort? They must be the most trusting people in the world." Thom ponders.

Then, his sarcasm kicks in. "Either that or they are expecting me to walk into something I am not supposed to, so they have an excuse to kill me later." In either case, he really has no choice but to obey at this point.

As he walks out to the hallway, he notices that it is just as blindingly white as the interrogation room. There is nothing on any of the doors to indicate what each one is. His curiosity tells him to open one just to see what's in it, but his brain tells him to keep his hands to himself unless he intends on losing something precious to him, like his head.

*

"Hey, Max." Violet says cheerfully as she peeks into Max's room.

"Hi, Violet."

"Why the long face?"

"Oh, nothing, just tired. You're killing me, you know."

"Why, thank you! I take that as a compliment. It is my absolute goal to push all of the trainees to their highest capacity. Otherwise, I wouldn't be doing my job correctly," Violet says with a wide smile.

"So, what's up?"

"Why does it always have to be something? Can't I just come by to say hi?"

"Um, no, you always have something to say when you visit," Max says with a straight face.

"Oh, now you are hurting my feelings, but you are right. I do have something to say. I think it will cheer you up."

"What is it?"

Violet runs up to him, grabs his arm like usual, and says, "Come on!" as she leads him out of the door down the corridor.

"Where are we going?"

"You will see."

As Violet drags him along, Max stares down the hallway and sees a familiar figure. "No, it cannot be him. Can it?" Max asks himself.

Thom's standing in the middle of the hallway, trying to figure out what he should do when he spots two people coming toward him.

Should he take his chances and try to ask them where he's supposed to be or should he lean flat against the wall so they can pass through? As he continues to ponder, his gaze falls on Max.

"Max?!" Thom shouts.

Stunned, Max stops and says, "It is you! Thom! What are you doing here?"

Thom steps forward and envelops Max in a large bear hug. They do a manly pat on the back before separating.

"Oh, man, am I glad to see you! I thought you were dead or something! I have been looking all over the place for you, buddy!" Thom says excitedly.

"I missed you, too, man!" Max replies.

Violet cannot believe how happy these two are to see each other. Trip's intuition was right. These two will do anything for one another and they are the key to winning this war.

Then, Thom notices Violet looking at him. After the hearty greeting, Thom looks at Violet and asks slyly. "And who is this pretty young thing? You disappear for a few days and I find you with a girl! You go, my man! So proud of you!" Laughing, Thom gives him another pat on the back.

Clearing his throat, Max looks at Thom and announces, "May I introduce Violet."

"Enchanté, mademoiselle," Thom says as he takes a bow. "My name is Thomas Richardson. It is a pleasure to meet your acquaintance."

Chuckling, Violet says, "Well, you are such a gentleman! It's nice to meet you, too!" Then, she looks at Max and says with a big smile, "Obviously, he doesn't know who I am."

Confused, Thom asks, "Am I missing something?"

Violet winks at Max as he says, "Otherwise known as the Warrior."

As expected, Thom takes a step back. "What?"

Both Violet and Max chuckle at Thom's dumbfounded expression.

"You look surprised. Do you know where you are, Thom?" Violet asks with an exaggerated expression of shock.

"If you are the Warrior, am I in the rebel headquarters?"

"Yup." Violet replies.

Then, he looks at Max and says, "And are you working for them?"

"Sort of, kind of." Max says.

"What kind of an answer is that?! Are you or aren't you?" Thom says loudly.

"Chill. There is no need to get overly excited." Violet says.

"It's complicated. I am not sure if I can explain it right now."

Letting out a deep breath, Thom says, "Give me a minute. This is a *lot* to take in," as he leans backward.

"Wait a minute, what are you doing here, Thom?" Max asks after thinking for a second.

Max is more than a little curious. Why in the world would the General of the Legion be in the rebel headquarters, just wandering around the hallways? It didn't make any sense whatsoever. He is not in handcuffs. Nor is he being watched by guards. It's as if he is just another member of the Desiderios. The last he checked, these two are at war with one another, aren't they?

"Well, apparently, this *sort of, kind of* thing that you got going on runs in the family. I just saw your Aunt Lillian outside. I think she is also *sort of, kind of* part of the rebellion, but said she isn't. I think she is the one who knocked me out."

"Aunt Lillian is here? I haven't seen her in ages! How is she doing?"

"She looks fine to me. Your Uncle Adam is with her."

"Awesome! Haven't seen him in a long time either! What about Sean? He is about, what, nine years old by now? I haven't seen him since he was a baby."

"Oh, I didn't see Sean."

Then, it hits him. "Wait, did you say she *knocked you out*?"

"Yup, that's what I said."

A shocked expression appears on Max's face. He never pictured Aunt Lillian or Uncle Adam as the violent type. From what he remembers, they rarely ever raised their voices, let alone lifted a hand to hit someone. What did Thom do to deserve getting hit?

Before he can open his mouth to ask again, Thom says with weary eyes, "That's a long story, too. It has been a very confusing and tiring couple of days since you disappeared."

After hearing those words, Max is touched that Thom is such a loyal best friend.

Then, Thom looks at him in anticipation and says, "Speaking of your disappearance, what happened to you? All I found was this black feather." Thom takes it out of his pocket to show it to Max.

"I don't know where the feather came from," Max says as he studies it. "But, I was shot with a dart. It may have come from that."

Those words pique Violet's curiosity. That's strange. Is Trip so careless that he would actually leave clues at the scene of the crime? After taking a closer look, she smiles. Nope, that's just some random feather that he found at the site.

She shakes her head. She cannot believe that she, at least for one second, doubted El Diablo's professionalism. He doesn't deserve that name if he's sloppy enough to leave something as obvious as that just lying around. On second thought, she is starting to think that he left it there on purpose to throw the enemies off. If he did, it worked wonders.

"Who shot you?" Thom asks.

Sensing that this is not a conversation that she wants them to have at this time, Violet interrupts and says, "Why don't we get out of the hallway and continue this discussion in a more comfortable setting?"

Then, she proceeds to drag Max down the hallway and opens the third door on the left.

"Hiya, Trip," Violet says. "I believe you remember Thom here."

Trip looks up while Thom, once again, looks confused and asks, "Have we met?"

Max looks at him and says, "Oh, boy, here we go again."

"This here is Trip," Violet says.

Thom gives him a lighthearted wave and says, "Hi, nice to meet you."

"Guess you haven't made the connection yet, huh," Violet says.

Thom continues to have a blank look on his face.

"Help him out here, Max," Violet says.

"If Violet is the Warrior, then Trip is….." Max says with a dramatic flair as he waits for Thom to respond.

"The Warrior and ….?" Max repeats it when nothing comes out of Thom's mouth.

"Wow, he *is* dense!" Violet says as she shakes her head.

Thom is looking at Trip. This man dressed in all black looks so confident and creepy at the same time. So, obviously, he is not a mere private. If the Warrior is here to introduce him personally, he must be someone important.

Wait a minute! "Is he El Diablo!?" Thom finally says as he thinks about it.

"Bravo! He finally got it!" Violet grins as she claps her hands.

Looking at the door to get ready for a quick exit, Thom asks, "Why have you brought me here?"

"Relax, he doesn't eat babies, contrary to whatever rumors that the Legion has spread out there. He's actually a very nice guy once you get to know him," Violet replies gleefully. Then, her tone changes and says, "Now that we are all here. Let's get down to business."

After having spent the last few days with her, Max knows that tone and quiets down immediately to listen to her.

"Why did you bring Max into the Legion?" Trip asks point blank.

"I wanted to take care of him," Thom answers.

As all three of them stare at him, Thom senses a gut wrenching feeling, as if he is in the middle of a horrible nightmare where he is naked standing in front of a crowd of people who are gawking and whispering to one another.

"You mean like the way you took care of his parents?" Violet asks sarcastically.

Before that moment, Max has never even entertained the possibility that Thom was maybe involved in the murder of his parents. He does not know what to expect. He is hoping against hope that he had nothing to do with it, but logically, how can he not?

"I don't understand. What does this have to do with his parents? I have never done anything to them." Thom replies.

Max is somewhat relieved to hear Thom's apparent ignorance, but he still wants to know the truth. If he does have something to do with it ... ugh, he cannot even fathom the possibility. For crying out loud, Thom loves Mom's cookies and Dad's jokes! How can he possibly have a hand in something so heinous!

"What have you learned from their journals?" Violet continues as she gives him a hint.

Max is surprised to hear about the journals, but keeps his silence, at least for the moment, until he hears what Thom has to say.

Looking a little embarrassed for having been busted, Thom looks at Max sheepishly and says, "Sorry, I found your journal in your room when you disappeared. I wasn't trying to invade your privacy. I swear!"

Max gives him a tight lipped smile, which sends a chill down Thom's spine. Even though his lips seem to say, "It's OK," his eyes are as cold as ever. He actually doesn't remember his friend ever looking at him like that before.

Even though Max is a little offended, he is not really surprised. He didn't exactly *hide* it. He simply put it out of sight. A part of him figured that Thom would find it and wanted his friend to know what he really thinks.

"Well, I am still waiting," Violet says as if she is a school teacher looking at a scared little boy who has no idea what the answer is.

Then, Thom realizes that it's time for him to man up and stop letting her treat him like a child. Even though he is only 18 years old, he is still a respected member of the Legion and should be treated accordingly. Regardless of whether or not he is the leader's son, he did bust his rear working up the ranks over the last five years. No matter what anyone else thinks, he knows that he deserves his position and he needs to start acting like a General.

Standing up straight and relaxing his arms, he says, "Look, I understand that all three of you may have a reason to be upset with me, but that does not mean that I need to take that condescending tone from you. I already told you I have nothing to do with his parents' disappearance."

"Well, looks like someone finally got his manhood back," Violet jokes.

Ignoring her, Thom continues, "Max, I read your parents' journals, too. Based on everything I have read, it's safe to say that your entire family is against the Legion. I am sorry to have dragged you into it. If I had known what I know now, I would not have put you in such an uncomfortable position."

"That's OK," Max replies half-heartedly. While he honestly wants to forgive his best friend, it's getting harder and harder to do so.

"I swear I am going to do everything I can to help you find your parents."

"This proves it," Violet says to Trip, "He is not in the know in the Legion headquarters."

Thom looks at his friend's face, which has turned ashen. "What's the matter? Did I say something wrong?"

"They're dead," Max says dryly as he looks at the floor.

"What? When did this happen?"

"If you read their journals, I am pretty sure you have an educated guess," Violet replies.

"I am really, really sorry, Max. I didn't know."

Max continues to stare at the floor. Their deaths have not completely sunk in yet. Even though his head knows that they are not coming back, he has not been able to grieve. All he gets is a throbbing headache every time he hears someone mention their deaths. It's as if he is going to explode any minute, but doesn't know how.

"Who did you put in charge at the Legion headquarters when you decided to come snooping around here?" Violet interrupts his thought.

"I wasn't snooping. I was following a hunch," Thom responds matter-of-factly.

"Where did you get this hunch from?"

"Where else? The same place that I have been using to try to piece together everything for the last few days."

"Ah, the journals."

"And before you become sarcastic again. The answer is General Hawk."

"There is that name again. What do you know of this General Hawk?"

"Well, he is an upstanding soldier. He's been in the Legion for the last 20 years and has earned many commendations for his heroism."

"Oh, you mean, he killed innocent civilians?" Violet retorts.

Trip shoots her a look. Even though he agrees with her statement, he is getting tired of listening to this sarcastic banter going back and forth and wants to get to the point already.

Violet gets the hint and says, "We don't need to hear about the fluff. We need to know how he operates and how he thinks."

"Do you honestly think I am going to tell you? I am still the General of the Legion. You really think I am going to betray my men? At least Adam had the good sense to threaten to cut off my finger before asking these types of questions."

"If that's what it takes, I am happy to oblige," Violet says as she snatches his wrist in an iron grip and brandishes her knife, holding it to his skin.

Both Max and Thom are in shock and neither one of them can decide if they are impressed or scared.

"If I take off your index finger, you won't be able to pull the trigger anymore. Maybe I should do that and make it easier on us. What do you think?"

Trip is as emotionless as always. There she goes again, showing off. He knows she isn't going to do anything rash. She's much more calculating than that.

Sweating a little, Thom says, "You think I am afraid? Do your worst! You know who my father is. He will definitely take his revenge personally if something happens to me."

"I think you give your father a little too much credit. He is always looking out for the number one person in his heart– himself."

Thom seethes with anger. "How dare you!"

"What? Don't like a dose of the truth?"

Trip cannot believe the lame lines that are coming out of her mouth, but, in a way, he is starting to enjoy the show. It's funny, really, knowing both the gentle and the fierce sides of her, to watch this little charade unfold. He already knows that she is going to win. She always does.

Struggling, Thom repeats himself, "Do what you want with me! Max will be my witness."

"What? You are actually going to bring your dear friend into your fight? Have you learned nothing? You realize Trip here can take off your head before you blink if he wants to, right?"

"So, why doesn't he do it?"

"If you behave, we will tell you."

Thom grimaces. Her grip is getting tighter with every word that comes out of her mouth. She's abnormally strong for a woman her size.

"Fine, fine! I will do what you ask."

"That's better." As Violet lets go of her grip, Thom hisses with pain and cradles his wrist. "OK, I am going to honor your desire to be loyal to your men – for now. So, I am going to ask you a different question. Does anyone know that you are here?"

"I didn't tell anyone in the Legion headquarters, if that's what you are asking."

"Besides the journals, is there another reason why you decided to come this way?"

Thom knows that there is. The reports often come in about the sightings in this area, but no one ever acts on it because it's difficult to carry weapons while climbing the mountains.

Not only that, but on the rare occasions when they're able to spare the men to search, they never find anyone. Now he knows that it's probably because the rebels have the home advantage and know every hiding place in the mountains.

"No," Thom replies.

"You've got to be kidding me. You are lying already!" Violet says in disgust.

"I am not!"

"Alright, you leave us no choice," Violet grabs Max's arm and heads towards the door.

As she turns towards Trip, she realizes that there is no point. He has already left. She rolls her eyes and says, "Typical."

Before Thom can comprehend what just happened, he hears the click of a lock.

"Did she? No! Did she just lock me in?" he exclaims aloud. Disbelief crosses his face as he tries in vain to open the door. "I cannot believe she did that."

He goes to the chair that Trip had been sitting on and plops down on it. This is the first time he actually looks around the room. It's completely white with a table and chairs, just like the interrogation room. The only difference is instead of a mirror across from him, there is a camera.

Was that a test? If it was, did he just fail? Is he a prisoner now? Ugh! Thom stands abruptly, causing the chair to fall over. He angrily paces the room, seething with anger by now.

*

"So, why are you doing this?" Max asks after they are a good distance from the room that holds Thom.

"I need to know that I can trust him." Violet replies.

"I don't see how you can. He is the General of the Legion. It's a little bit much to expect him to turnaround so fast."

"You did."

"I am sure you know that there is a world of difference between my situation and his."

"Is there?" Violet asks rhetorically as she raises her eyebrow.

"I don't understand. How can you compare me to him? Our ranks are opposite of one another. Our fathers, well, you know." Max cannot get himself to finish that sentence.

"I know," Violet replies with an understanding smile. "All of that may be true, but I think it's time you learn a little bit more about your parents' past." Then, she takes out Philip's and Sonya's journals and hands them to him. "I am sure you will find them to be very interesting reading."

"Are these what I think they are?"

"Yes, happy reading." Violet says before taking off.

*

As she approaches the garden, Violet sees Trip taking a whiff of his roses.

"It's nice to see your gentle side."

Trip ignores her and continues to tend his flowers.

"Well, if you have nothing to say, I am going to go first. I think we are on track. Max is reading the journals, and Thom is where we want him to be. By this time tomorrow, we should have them both on our side."

"Good."

Chapter 10: The Beginning

Just like Thom, Max is completely entrenched in the journals once he starts to read them. He never knew that his parents had once worked for the Legion. Apparently, they took the word confidential very seriously. Neither one of them have ever mentioned who they worked for, let alone what the projects are. As a child, he never really cared what they did for a living. All he knew was that his parents were hard working people who went to work every day and made a good living. In this respect, at least, Max and Thom are not that different after all.

Unlike Thom who was somewhat envious of Mrs. Sullivan's affectionate words, Max is a little bit embarrassed. It's just a little too mushy for a child to read. Nevertheless, he reads every word, not wanting to miss anything that his Mom has to say now that she is no longer around to be able to tell him in person. Before long, Max has finished reading about his Mom's resignation from the Legion. The next entry starts to get a little more cryptic.

*

February 28, 2084

It's a glorious day today. It's still a little brisk but the sky is blue and everything is wonderful! It has become so clear to me now — what my purpose in life is. Besides having Max, this is what Philip and I are destined to do. I am so excited! Now, I know I can do something in this world that can make a difference.

That's great. This entry says absolutely nothing to Max. Even though it alludes to the possibility that she has become acquainted with elements of the underground or at least had a discussion with someone who may have gotten her excited about her future, there is no real information to go on. There is no name, place, not even a hint of any kind.

That would be Mom. She can be excited about something that she cannot talk about. But, that doesn't stop her from bragging about it!

*

March 16, 2084

Well, this has been an interesting day. Even though Philip and I were not born into families that can be called upper class, by being smart with money, we have been blessed with the ability to travel extensively. During which time, I have seen some pretty remarkable things in my day. We even made the point of visiting all Seven Wonders of the World. And, each is truly deserving of its title!

Yet, what I saw today takes the cake. I met a new friend and he showed me his "home", well, to use that term loosely. It's an incredible maze. I never knew where I would end up. If you don't know where you are going, you can end up going in circles for hours! It's kind of fun, actually. It's an adventure at every turn. Of course, like all forms of explorations, not every one of them is pleasant. Occasionally, we would meet with a not so pleasant smell or less than desirable critters.

Some of the turns end up in dead ends where our host introduced some of his other "roommates". They are all so sincere and honest. It's quite refreshing. Often when we meet new people, they try to be polite because they want to make a good first impression. Obviously, there is nothing wrong with that. After all, who doesn't want to make a good first impression? The only problem is I have often met ones that are so fake that it can be uncomfortable to be in their presence.

On the other hand, some of the people we met today can also be too brutally honest. For example, one guy told me that he thought my hair was too long. If he had stopped at that, it would have been perfectly fine. Everyone is entitled to his or her own opinion, right? Well, he kept on going. He continued to criticize other features, such as my makeup. He then proceeded to take a pair of scissors and a dirty rag towel as if he was going to cut my hair and wipe the makeup off my face right there and then! Talk about rude!

Oh, well, Philip put a stop to that pretty quickly. He is such a sweetheart! In any case, this is not going to deter us from continuing on with our life's missions. In fact, I am looking forward to it more than ever!

*

Well, this entry is less secretive than the previous one. It's pretty clear that the home that she's referring to is not really a private residence. He has never seen one with mazes that can confuse visitors. So, this seems to be the first time that she references the underground, at least physically.

She's also insinuating that members of the rebellion can be too blunt for their own good. So much so that both of Max's parents seemed to have taken offense to some of their actions.

This observation seems to be pretty consistent with his experiences with the underground rebels. Just thinking about how that jerk had insisted that Max made a mistake when he was the one who was not listening still riles him up a little. Apparently, just because you are on the same team does not mean that they have to be nice to you, which does not give Max a warm, fuzzy feeling about the group.

What happens in time of war? Will he be able to trust any of them with his life? He shudders to think what would happen if there's an occasion where his life is in their hands.

Unlike El Diablo and the Warrior in the rebel headquarters, some of the rebels underground seem to just be plain frustrated and crude. So, they often say whatever comes to mind without thinking it through first. That's too bad because some of these foul mouthed rebels are really good fighters who are loyal believers of their cause.

Wonder what caused them to be so bitter, besides the fact that they have been fighting a war for the last six years and there does not seem to be an end in sight? Do Trip and Violet know about them?

Considering that they are such genuine people themselves, it stands to reason to think that they do. More importantly, will the frustration boil over and become a problem for the Desiderios as a whole?

Well, no point reminiscing or asking those questions right now.

*

June 18, 2084

My suspicions have been right all along. Somebody is making things up. It really angers me to know that someone can be so callous and create rumors that put people in harm's way. What kind of animal would do such a thing? I would love to catch them and make them stop doing these heinous deeds.

*

This is the first time that his mother has hinted at what her job in the underground is. It sounds very much like the same thing that she was doing for the Legion. So, in a way, she can thank the Legion for having given her the real life experience that she needed in order to be effective at her job for the rebels.

If Victor had known about this turn of events, he was sure to be unhappy with it and would have regretted making her an intelligence officer.

After all, he was the one who personally invited them into the Legion. So, he is guilty of one of two things. He is either a horrible judge of character for believing that Max's parents would be good assets for the Legion, or he made a grievous mistake in helping the rebels. Either case, he is in the wrong in more ways than one.

In order to correct his mistakes, it is very possible that Victor is the one who is responsible for the Sullivans' deaths.

The next few entries are more of the same cryptic messages about people she has met and more places that she has seen. Each time, Mrs. Sullivan is very careful not to include any names or information that can lead the reader to the location that she's referring to in her journal.

She often refers to everyone as a friend and almost never includes any form of description. There are some cases where she would include specifics such as their height or age, but that is about the extent of the details that she would write. Then, Max comes across a different entry.

*

December 21, 2084

Things are getting worse in the Dominion. It seems that every day is filled with bad news. The citizens of Balavan are becoming increasingly dissatisfied.

There has been an increasing number of crimes happening in the dominion ranging from petty theft to murders, and there are simply not enough police officers to handle it. It's so sad. Even the reporters seem to be on edge.

This used to be a nice dominion. People were always laughing and enjoying themselves. There were plenty of wonderful restaurants, shops, and theatres. Stadiums and concerts were always filled with adoring fans. For those who prefer relaxation, there were also numerous parks to visit and challenging trails to hike.

Now, the nice stores are closing, most probably because the owners fear being targeted. Even the theatres and stadiums are now empty, and the lakes are filled with trash.

If something is not done about it soon, chaos is going to erupt. I can feel it. And it's not going to be pleasant. We have to be ready for anything – especially for our children's sake.

*

Children? Since Max is an only child, it is pretty obvious that his mother is not just talking about him, but children all around the dominion. As a youth, Max knew something was going on, but his parents did a marvelous job of keeping the unpleasant news away from the youngsters and tried to make life seem as normal as possible.

Thom continued to come by his house and they went to school like normal. Max's mother continued to bake cookies and throw birthday parties while his father always acted relaxed at home. They both knew that if they acted agitated, the children would sense it.

Then again, by shielding Max from bad news, was she doing the same thing that Victor was? Isn't she also trying to influence him? After thinking for a moment, Max concludes that the answer is no. Her intentions were different, which makes all the difference in the world. From this entry, it certainly sounds like Victor used the news as the seed to start the war.

Hence, unlike Victor who was manipulating the news by putting out bad news when he wants to agitate the public and good news when he wants them to be in peace, his mother only told him good news to protect him. No matter if it is right or wrong, Max feels better now that he has a valid rationale for his mother's actions. As Max continues reading, he sees an entry that seems odd but very intriguing.

*

June 24, 2085

Guess what? I received a phone call from an old friend today. It was Victor, Thom's father. It's a rare treat. Neither Philip nor I have seen or heard from him for many years. I think the last time we saw him was back before we even started working for the Legion. Yes, it's been that long. I am sure of it. He didn't really say what he wanted but just said hi, which, to say the least, is a little unusual.

It almost seems as if he was checking up on us. Since we were pretty much taken by surprise, we didn't really have anything to say to him. I hope he doesn't think that we were being rude. After all, both of our children remain best friends. We should be at least cordial to one another.

Max doesn't remember either one of his parents mentioning this phone call. Usually, if it has something to do with Thom, they would have mentioned it.

For example, he remembers one time when Thom won an award for rookie of the year in his football team. His mother was so happy for him that she invited him over for a little celebratory party to congratulate him on being such a great athlete.

In other words, Max's mother must have thought that the phone call was suspicious enough to keep it to herself and her private journal instead of sharing with anyone else – even those she can trust. Despite the seemingly casual entry, it's possible that she believed the mere knowledge of the call taking place could put the recipient of this information in potential danger of some sort.

If that is the case, she must have been afraid of Victor and was well aware of his reputation and his ability to destroy his enemies. Having association with the underground would make the Sullivans an enemy of the Legion.

*

July 28, 2085

Great, the crime wave seems to have finally reached the countryside. Philip spotted a trespasser on our estate this afternoon.

When he confronted him, the man claimed that he was lost on his way to his aunt's house in the neighborhood. He thought he could find it faster by walking across our property. Unfortunately, it's pretty obvious that he was lying since we know all of our neighbors and he couldn't tell us who he was really visiting.

Philip looked around the estate. Even though nothing seems to be missing, he found several disturbances.

There are signs that someone was digging up our land looking for things. We are not sure what they can possibly be looking for underground, but they did not do a very good job of covering their tracks. They practically ruined our flower gardens. Philip also noticed that some of our wires have been tampered with. It took him hours to trace them to make sure that the house is still safe to live in, but this is definitely not a good sign.

*

Max remembers those days right before the war started. Everyone in school was scared, including the teachers and the principals. There were armed guards manning every door and metal bars on every window. As soon as the bell rang, all of the doors were in lock down.

Back then, Max had wondered whether or not the emergency exits would be able to handle all of the people in the school if a fire or other disaster happened. The locks and gates would have stopped them from being able to leave. Thankfully, he never had to find out.

It's amazing that anyone was able to concentrate in class at all during those days. It seemed like every day, there was a new tragic event happening in town. On the other hand, what the school officials did not realize at the time is that they were never really in any danger.

For some strange reason, the war has been and continues to be fought strictly within the dominion. Any damage occurring outside of the dominion is merely incidental or accidental. The Sullivans' estate in the country is mostly unscathed, of course, so is the Richardson'

160

mansion as well as the residences of the higher ranking officers in the Legion. All of which are outside the borderline of Balavan. Within the dominion, however, the devastation increased every day. It's as if the war was only about capturing the dominion itself.

But that fact is not the only curious thing about this entry. After all, consider the timing. Roughly one month after Victor's mysterious phone call, men are seen on the Sullivans' estate snooping around and putting up surveillance equipment. Although there's a one in a million chance that this is a coincidence, it certainly looks like Victor is behind all of this.

*

October 13, 2085

This is it! We have reached the point of no return. The unthinkable has happened. Someone has murdered the Sovereign of Balavan! Despite all of the security around his mansion, he was reportedly killed in his own bed by an intruder. The police have no suspects, but as always, rumors are rampant.

Word on the street is a rebel disguised as a maid snuck into his chambers and slashed his throat while he slept. How horrible! Not to speak ill of the dead, but if he had put in more effort to stop the crimes instead of worrying about his own mansion, he may have avoided this tragedy. But, alas, it is too late.

*

That was the day before the Legion declared war against the rebels. The death of Sovereign Carson became the impetus to start the fight. Many people, especially the rebels, have suspected that the Legion may have been the ones who actually killed Carson and started the rumors so the residents would side with them.

As many rumors are, there is strong suspicion that this one also has no merit. Due to the increase in crime, Carson had installed hidden cameras in every room, recording every entrance in real time. To make sure that it was completely secure, he gave specific instructions that only members of security know about them. In addition, in order for anyone to enter mansion, he or she must have a retinal scan, which is also recorded and reviewed by the security team.

After his death, the police combed through volumes of the recordings and have found no evidence of any unauthorized entries. At least that was what the official announcement indicated. There were no broken windows, no warning alarms going off, and no suspicious characters roaming the hallways.

In other words, it was most probably an inside job. Being paranoid about his own safety, he hired the best security guard; most of them current members of the Legion who were moonlighting.

Even now, the police continue to investigate, but although the police have not ruled out anyone, they are also not naming any names. It's possible that they are afraid of being targeted if they do. Or, it is also possible that the police simply do not care to catch the real culprit.

After all, Carson's lies, corruption, and selfishness didn't exactly make him the most popular person in the realm. Even those who stand to gain the most by having him in their pockets no longer cared for him since he no longer had any real power over the people.

Meanwhile, mass exodus of its residents began on that day. Those who could afford to leave earlier had already done so months ago. Over the next few weeks, the dominion lost about one-third of its population. While some merely moved to the countryside, others have gone far, far away. By that time, everyone knew that war is inevitable. They just didn't realize that it was the eve of war.

*

October 16, 2085

The war has begun. There is shooting all around the dominion, day and night. It's absolutely atrocious. Even though we are about ten miles away from the dominion, we can hear the constant barrage of shelling and see flashes of light throughout the night. It's quite disheartening.

I know Max is worried. I can see it in his eyes, but, like always, he is a champ and does not express it openly. He is probably taking a cue from us. What a sweetheart! His friend Thom has not visited us as often since the war started. Wonder how his family is doing and what they are thinking?

*

By 6AM on October 14, 2085, the first shots were fired and the shells discharged, effectively waking up everyone within a 5 mile radius. Nobody knows who started it, but it was smack in the middle of the dominion. They could not have picked a more populated place, as if it was a warning signal to everyone saying: *get out now if you value your lives!*

As soon as it started, it seemed to keep going. Unlike the battles back in the day that often ended within 30 minutes because there would not be any more men left to fight on the battlefield, the battles in this war go on much longer.

The first battle of the war showed just how deadly the weapons both sides handled were.

Despite the obvious destruction in the middle of town, no one was able to tell where the shots were coming from because they were all being fired or detonated from a distance.

Being the official protectors of the dominion, the Legion was quick to broadcast what they called a cowardly act by the Desiderios. Max has yet to hear what Trip's take is on the beginning of the war, but he is pretty sure that the official announcement is a little more than biased.

The rebels never bothered to issue any form of statement in response to the Legion's character assassination. As far as they were concerned, the Legion was merely trying to incite them enough to get them to make a mistake in a public forum.

Violet is way too smart for that and Trip cares way too little for those tactics to be suckered into such a cheap gimmick.

*

October 28, 2085

Philip and I are obviously concerned. We are doing everything we can to help out, but it's not really up to us. And it is a lot more difficult than we had initially anticipated.

*

It seems that the shorter the entry, the more Max's mother is trying to say, but cannot. This is a prime example.

It's only three short sentences, but, as far as Max is concerned, each one has a meaning. The first one indicates that both of his parents are involved in the war effort. Since they resigned from the Legion, it is safe to say that they are working for the Desiderios.

In the second sentence, Max believes it means his parents are probably not getting the full support that they need to do their jobs in the underground.

Finally, the third sentence hints that there may even be an obstacle in their way. Perhaps, there may be a mole that is spreading the rumors or sabotaging their efforts.

Knowing that his parents were killed while meeting a contact within the Legion, it is highly probable that a mole leaked their plans, which led them to a trap. If that is the case, Max is determined to find out whom.

*

December 2, 2085

The war has been going on for six weeks now. The Legion has placed the blame on the rebels, causing many residents of Balavan to accuse one another of being a member of the now infamous guerilla group. It's too bad, really, since there has been no proof that they started the war and most of the citizens have no idea what the war is even about. Instead, they simply think that the rebels are trying to overthrow the Legion because they want to take over the dominion and enslave its citizens.

Such accusations are kind of funny, actually. When was the last time that anyone in Balavan has been a slave? We have always prided ourselves on being very democratic. Yet, the people blindly believe what they hear on the news, like sheep. Sadly, they are completely unaware of the fact that the shepherd intends on leading them to slaughter.

So, if Max read that correctly, his mother was trying to say that the Legion was the one who started the war, but conveniently placed the blame on the Desiderios. Yet, she did not mention the group by name. Isn't it obvious who they are? After all, El Diablo and the Warrior did not just get their nicknames overnight.

Almost as soon as the war started, they built up their reputation as the terrifying fighters that they are. Is his mother hinting that there may be a third faction in the midst that is causing trouble? No, it cannot be, can it?

At the same time, the Legion doesn't seem to care who gets hurt in the process. In fact, it seems that she was saying that they expected casualties. Victor certainly deserves the name of the shepherd that his mother was referring to. He seems to be the one pulling all of the strings in the background. Even his beloved son is in the dark about his motives or even his next steps.

Of course, if Victor is the shepherd, that would make Thom the sheepdog. Max smiles at the thought. It's funny to think of his best friend as a canine. After all, isn't a dog often called a man's best friend? But, seriously, the more important question here is where is the shepherd going with them?

As far as Max can tell, there is no greener pasture that Victor can lead them to. Balavan was already a great dominion prior to the war. In addition, the dominion is in no danger of any sort. All of the small towns and tribes in the area have already been destroyed or chased out. Even when they were around, none of them were ever strong enough to be a threat. Now, Balavan is surrounded by nothing but the natural defenses of mountains and bodies of water. In other words, it is essentially in the perfect state.

After thinking for a few minutes, no matter how much Max wants to deny it, Victor seems to be defending his homeland more than anything else. If that's the case, that would make the Desiderios the bad guys. In his mind, that just cannot be.

Wait, Max finally realizes what he has been thinking of all this time. The dominion is *perfect* because the Legion thinks they have conquered everyone, but if that were true, everyone should be living the utopian life. There should be no rebellion if that was the case.

But the discontent spreading in the more recently conquered areas says that it is not as he thinks. In other words, even though Victor has destroyed their identities and their homes, he has failed to shatter their resolve.

Could it be that it was just the opposite? Could he have strengthened their resolve instead?

Actually, was it possible that he hadn't gotten rid of all of the natives? It was hard to catch everyone. Maybe someone had gotten away?

He reflected back on his interactions with the people of the rebellion. They were a very diverse group, almost as though they'd been thrown together in a pile without any sorting.

Like they'd come from different places.

Could it be that they were actually the ones that were thrown out of the dominion? Were they the original inhabitants of these lands?

It made sense; why else would they fight so much among each other?

They all had their own customs and traditions that they followed. Maybe some of those clashed with each other, and that was why they would be so rude as to try to cut off his mother's hair and wipe her makeup off.

They were definitely rough around the edges, but it was because they were rubbed the wrong way. Already different from each other, they were then pushed out of their homeland and forced to fight for it back.

They had to watch as they were taken over and went into hiding. They suffered though so many things.

Was that why his parents were so involved in the cause?

They found out what the rebels' true intentions are. They wanted to help them take back what was originally theirs. They would right the wrongs that had been done to them.

"Wow…" Max lies back on his bed, staring straight up into the ceiling, unblinking, taking in all he'd just learned.

It was unbelievable.

Chapter 11: Round Three

After Thom is left alone in the room, he starts to calm down. There is nothing left to do anyways. The room is void of everything except for a couple pieces of furniture. There isn't even a clock or a glass of water, let alone a bed. So, he lies down on the floor staring into the ceiling as he ponders about his trip so far and tries to make sense of what has just happened to him.

On the other hand, he is thankful that he has his watch with him. At least he knows what time it is. As expected, Violet had removed all other forms of electronics and tools from him, including his phone and compass. After making sure there were no tracking devices on his timepiece, she allowed him to keep it.

He sighs and glances at his wrist. It's almost 8PM and none of them have returned.

Just when he is starting to wonder if they are going to leave him in the room to rot, the door unlocks. Even though his first instinct is to ambush the poor person coming through the door, he changes his mind.

Not knowing the exits and not having anything on him that can help him escape, knocking out one person in the rebel headquarters would only get him into deeper trouble. He should know, because he would certainly chain up anyone who dares to knock him out if he was in their place.

"Good evening. I hope you are hungry! I don't know what you like. So, I played it safe and made you a cheeseburger and fries. Just don't tell me you are a vegetarian," a jolly woman says cheerfully.

It is Holloway, the rebel chef who can usually tell what someone wants to eat just by watching him for a few minutes. In this case, since she has not had the chance to spend any time with him, she had to make an educated guess based on what she knows about him.

"Oh, no. Thank you. It smells delicious. I am famished!" Thom says. As he is about to wolf down the meal and drink the tall glass of water, he pauses for a moment and looks at her, who is smiling at him.

"Don't worry. It's not poisoned," she says with a grin. "If El Diablo wanted to kill you, he would have done it a long time ago."

"No, that's not what I was thinking," Thom says, then grimaces as he hears the hesitation in his own voice.

Holloway gives him an understanding smile before taking her leave.

After enjoying his dinner, the door unlocks again. This time, Holloway brings Clay with her.

Thom adopts a wary stance once he catches sight of the eerily pale man, but the man barely gives him a glance before setting down a sack he's carrying in front of Thom.

Holloway retrieves the dishes before saying, "Have a good night!" and locks the door back up.

Opening the sack, Thom sees a nice fluffy sleeping bag, a pillow, a pair of pajamas, and an assortment of men's clothing.

"That is very thoughtful of them!" Thom thinks aloud as he lets out a slight smile. He picks up different shirts and pants to see which one he prefers. Like his friend Max, he picks a bright shirt and black pants, folds them nicely, and places them on the table. He then proceeds to fold up the rest of the clothes and put them in a neat little pile.

Watching him from the security camera, Violet says, "See that! He picked an outfit that looks so similar to what Max picked! I really think he and Max are twins."

*

"Good morning, sunshine!" Max hears the all too familiar cheerful voice that has become his most reliable alarm clock.

Without opening his eyes, he responds, "Good morning, Violet. Give me a minute and I will be ready for your abuse."

"Haha, that's so hilarious. Meet you out in exactly 60 seconds or you will regret it."

"Oh, man!" Max knows she is dead serious when she says something like that. She should have said give me *five* minutes, not *a* minute! He jumps right out of bed instantly, changes his clothes, puts on his shoes, and out the door he goes. It's better to skip the shower and the teeth brushing this morning. Bad hygiene is definitely a better alternative than the tough day he would have if he is late.

He comes to an abrupt stop when he spots her leaning against the wall right outside of his door, laughing hysterically. "Very good, soldier! 53 seconds flat. You have a whole 7 seconds to spare. Good Job!"

He nods at her, still a little breathless from the rushing he had to do.

Instead of carrying all of the weapons this time, Violet has left it by the wall, which Max wisely understands to mean that it's his turn to do the heavy lifting. The only problem is he hadn't expected it to be so heavy! As Violet walks down the hallway in her usual quick pace, Max tries to catch up.

"Let's go!" Violet says as she smiles at Max who is half walking and half limping with his back hunched over as he tries to carry the load as quickly as he can.

Every day, Max is more and more amazed at what Violet can do. Over the past few days, he has wondered how much weight she can carry. Today, Max is more than impressed with the answer to that question. Despite her small frame, she is so much stronger than she looks.

"OK, I am going to give you a little break here," Violet says as she stops at a door and knocks.

When she doesn't hear an answer, she knocks again and says, "I hope you are decent!" before unlocking the door and opening it with a slam to announce their arrival.

"Huh? What happened? What's going on?" Thom shouts as he sits up from the sleeping bag. He frantically scans around the room looking as confused as ever.

"Good morning, Thom," Max says after he dumps the heavy cargo in the room.

"Max? Where am I?"

"Remember? This young lady over here locked you in this room last night?"

Thom blinks as he looks at Violet, "Oh, yeah. Good morning, Warrior. Can I go now?"

"If you mean whether or not you can get out of this room, the answer is yes."

"It's about time!" Thom says as he hops up and starts getting ready to leave.

"Not so fast, buddy," Violet says as she holds her hand out.

"What? You said I can leave."

"Yes, but just because you can get out of this room does not mean you can just wander off wherever you wish."

"Oh," Thom says with a disappointed expression on his face.

172

"It's OK," Max consoles him with a pat on the shoulder. "It's not as bad as it sounds. Well, at least not this part anyways."

"What do you mean?" Thom gives him a curious look.

"Oh, you will see," Max says with a devilish grin.

"If you two are done chit chatting. Let's go. Times a wasting!" Violet declares.

Max nods and picks up the gear before following her. Thom reluctantly follows suit.

*

"Well, we're here. The rules are simple – everyone for himself." Looking at Thom, Violet says, "Now, show me what you got!"

Max knows exactly what she means. He picks up a rifle and runs for the trees. Violet takes off into the bushes and disappears.

Before Thom realizes it, he is standing there by himself. Oh, Crap! They obviously know something that he doesn't.

Not one to be slow, he picks up the cue and follows suit. This is obviously some sort of training or a test of his abilities.

Unlike Max who picks up one heavy weapon, however, he scans his selection quickly and gets three different ones.

Crouching on a branch high above Thom's head with a clear view of him, Violet watches him make his choices quickly and efficiently. She is impressed at how fast he thinks on his feet in the battlefield.

"Smart man. I guess he does deserve his title in the Legion after all," she says to herself. Instead of going after

Thom in full force the way she did with Max, she decides to lie in waiting; much like a lioness would to her prey.

Max was easy. His prior training consisted of mostly just shooting. While he is very good at it, he has not learned the art of war. He was merely lying in wait for his target, completely oblivious of everything else.

That is why it was so easy for Trip to capture him. In fact, none of the sharpshooters were aware of their surroundings. So much so that no one even noticed Trip's presence even after Max was abducted.

He could have easily taken every one of them out within minutes without anyone ever seeing him. That would have been a shrewd move on his part if he did. After all, sharpshooters are some of the most important soldiers for the Legion. Without them, they would be without the element of surprise on the battlefield. Because sharpshooting is not an easy thing to train, it would have taken them months to retrain a new team, giving the Desiderios a distinct advantage.

But, that was not Trip's mission at the time. He is a very focused man, especially on the battlefield. The last thing he wants is a distraction and deviation from the plan is considered one. Unless there is a very compelling reason, he almost never strays from his task at hand.

That is not to say that he does not think while he is on a mission or improvise when needed. On the contrary, he is always thinking, but no one can tell because of his gloomy nonchalant attitude. He just likes to keep his thoughts to himself, not even telling his best friend.

What he was thinking when he took Max was that there is no point killing the sharpshooters because they could be good assets later. At the time, he did not have the time nor the resources to assess which ones were worthy of capture. So, he chose to leave them alone.

At least, that is what Violet thinks. Wait, why is she thinking about Trip now? This is no time to be distracted. Even if it's just a training session, she needs to be serious.

"OK, snap out of it. You've got a job to do." Violet chastises herself.

She shakes her head and tells herself that she needs to focus on her new trainee now. This may be a difficult task.

Thom is almost the polar opposite of his friend. He has much more experience with field training. Thom is not as easy to spot. Ironic, really. The sniper is not as good at hiding as the man who must be seen by all of his men in order to lead.

She wants to study this one and see how he works. She can already tell that he has been training very hard over the last five years. Despite being so young, he carries himself like he has been fighting on the battlefield his entire life. Of course, having been training since she was five years old, Violet is better than any of them – if she puts her mind into it.

Scanning the area, she has already spotted Max. He is hiding behind a large tree trunk. It looks as if he is getting dangerously close to a patch of poison ivy, and he looks completely oblivious of that fact. But, hey, what's a few rashes when you are in the heat of battle, right?

Violet smiles and says to herself, "Note to self: do not come in contact with Max until he washes himself. No need to mess up *this* pretty skin."

As she continues to survey the area, she senses a movement behind her and jumps out of the way just in time. A dagger lodges itself into the tree inches from her face. A glance in the direction it came from gives her a glimpse of Thom before he ducks away.

Not bad, not bad. She grins excitedly. It's time for her to step up her game. This one might actually be challenging.

With that, she disappears.

For a second, Thom is proud of himself for having found her, but that's merely a fleeting moment. As soon as her gaze falls on him, he knows she's seen him.

As soon as the session started, he already figured out that he needed to do one thing that Max didn't do on his first time out – camouflage himself.

Although they both selected bright shirts because they were not told about this training session, Thom was quick to smear mud all over his shirt the first moment he could. He also did not hesitate to cover his face and arms. Unlike Max, he knew the outdoors well enough to notice which plants to avoid and what could be used to camouflage himself.

He also knew Violet's tactic. Since it's everyone for himself, that means she may be hiding in wait for him to attack first in an attempt to draw her out. If he attacked her, it would be a one-on-one fight out in the open.

From the death grip that she had used earlier on him, he already knows that she is far stronger than she appears at first glance. He probably wouldn't be able to beat her in a head-on fight. Thom is not about to give her the satisfaction of attacking first, which gives Max the advantage.

When Violet ducked out of the way earlier, Max was able to catch a glimpse of her and hear the sound of the leaves rustling as a dagger flew through the woods. At that moment, he knew which direction she was in. Max also deduced that Thom was not that far away if he was the one who threw it at her.

"Yes! I got them!" Max thinks to himself.

He has never been able to find Violet in any of the sessions. Instead, he has been the target every single time and knows that it is time that he makes some progress.

Quietly, he makes his way toward the direction the sound came from while looking around for the other two.

Whoosh! It takes less than a second for Max to step on a hidden trap and go flying into the air. A cry escapes his lips as he's dragged upward, and he loses his grip on his rifle. He groans, hanging upside down. How could he have not seen that?

It was right there. Violet had made the traps beforehand, without much time, so it wasn't even that well hidden.

Even though he was watching for the enemy, he completely neglected the surroundings.

"Haha! Amateur! One down, one to go." Violet smiles as she congratulates herself for having taken down one. She knew Max was watching and that he would fall for such an easy trick. He definitely needs more work. While Max has fallen for every one of her traps so far, Thom has yet to be deceived by any of them.

Sensing that the sun is about to come up, she no longer wants to play the cat and mouse game. Stepping out into the open with weapons in both hands, she is ready for Thom's attack, but she senses none. "Great, he still wants to play. Alright, I guess I have to initiate."

Without moving a step, she closes her eyes and listens carefully. Instantly, she shoots into the woods without ever looking and continues to shoot several times in a calculated pattern before she hears a rustling sound.

Several footsteps moved but stopped soon enough. He was hiding somewhere.

She walks over to the sound, slowly canvassing the area, silent as a mouse. She searches for any signal of his presence, and it doesn't take long before she hears breathing, faster and harsher than that of a calm person.

He's nervous and right behind those bushes at 9 o'clock.

Violet smiles slowly. Gotcha.

She slowly leans down and then fires one shot right down the middle.

A groan resonates in the air and she parts the plants to see Thom, defeated.

"Are you alright?" Violet says with a smile. There is no blood or any outward sign of injury, but he is groaning in pain on the ground. "I will give you a minute and you can walk it off."

With that, Violet cuts Max down from the net and says, "You know what to do." before taking her leave to the dining hall for her usual breakfast.

Although she won, she is very impressed at the extent that she had to go through in order to take Thom down. She is satisfied that he has passed the initial test and does not need the same type of training that Max does. In fact, she is contemplating letting Thom do the training from now on, which would give her a few extra hours of beauty sleep. That is, if she can trust him. So far, she is not convinced that he is not going to run back to his father and tell him everything.

*

After dusting himself off, Max looks at his friend who is still huffing on the ground and says, "Seriously, are you alright?"

"Yeah, that woman sure knows her aim." Thom says somewhat bitterly.

Snickering a little, his friend says, "I am sorry, man. She has never hit me there before. Look on the bright side. This means that you challenged her enough to make her hit you below the belt, literally. I, on the other hand, still get the kid gloves."

"Sure, try to turn it into something positive. Only you can do that." Thom replies grumpily.

Helping his friend up, they both walk towards the dining hall.

*

"Hello, there, welcome!" Violet announces. "I know you guys probably have had your share of newcomers lately, but I have another one to introduce you to."

Everyone turns towards Thom as he and Max walk in. Instantly, some of the men recognize him. They jump up, quickly brandishing their weapons, ready to kill the enemy.

"Put down your weapons, fellows. It's okay. There is no need to panic. By the reaction in this room, I see he needs no introduction, but I am going to introduce him anyways. Everyone, this is Thom Richardson, General of the Legion."

"Why is he walking around freely?" Clay asks as he flashes his dagger slowly.

"Oh, simmer down. Did you not see the way he walked in? He is hardly walking freely," Violet says as she laughs.

"What did you do to him?"

"Not much. Just shot him in the groin with a pellet gun. Nothing is broken, except maybe his ego."

While she may not have shot him with real bullets, she'd still been using a military grade gun that packs quite a punch – literally.

"Well, I don't like it," Fisher replies.

"There is nothing to not like. He will be a member of the Desiderios soon enough."

At her announcement, everyone looks at Violet, including Thom.

"What are you talking about?" Wolfe barks. "How can you expect him to just turn around and become one of us?"

"You will see," Violet replies as she looks at Thom with a smile.

Thom is as confused as everyone else. What possesses her to think that he would turn his back on his men, especially his father? Is she planning on blackmailing me? Or is she going to extort me? Either case, I cannot turn my back on family! But, sensing that she and Max are the only ones who do not want to kill him right now, he keeps his opinion to himself.

As usual, Holloway comes by to give everyone their food. When she reaches Thom, she says, "Hello, again. I think it's time I formally introduce myself. I am Holloway."

Thom says, "Yes, I remember you. Thank you for being so kind. As you probably already know, I am Thom Richardson."

"What would you like today?"

Thinking for a second, Thom smiles and says, "How about a pack of ice for starters?"

At the sound of his request, the room fills with laughter. Violet looks around at everyone. They all seem to have calmed down a little. Although they still look suspicious of what is going on, they are no longer alarmed.

Maybe this is going to work out after all. She looks at Trip. Even though he is not laughing, he looks relatively relaxed, which is also a good sign.

After finishing her meal, Violet looks at Max and says, "Take good care of him, unless you want one of these guys to kill him."

Then, she winks and takes her leave.

*

Putting her feet on the conference room table, Violet casually asks Trip, "So, what do you think?"

"He is very good, but can be dangerous."

"Why?"

"He looks very loyal."

"Why is that a bad thing?"

"Isn't it obvious?"

"Well, yes, I know he's a boy scout but he is also a reasonable man."

"He's no Max."

"I know that. He needs a little more work, but I am up for a little challenge," Violet says confidently.

"What have you got in mind?"

"You will see."

"You know that time is of the essence."

"You can count on me. You know that."

Trip leaves it at that. He knows that she does these things very differently from him. Knowing that Violet is just testing the waters, there is no point continuing this conversation.

That is how she works. She doesn't simply fly by the seat of her pants. She thinks well when she has a muse. Instead of coming up with ideas beforehand, she likes to see where everything stands first before deciding on a unique solution to each problem.

There are two reasons for this tactic. First, no one will be able to sabotage her plans because they won't know her next move ahead of the time if she doesn't know it herself. Second, without formal military training, she never learned the best strategies for different situations. She has always had to figure it out as she goes. Eventually, that became the norm and she continued with it.

Within minutes, the rest of the team enters the room.

"Hey, guys. What did we miss?" Sunny starts off the discussion.

"Nothing. We were just chatting." Violet responds. Looking at Garret, she says, "What's new?"

Taking out his charts, he says, "We have intelligence that shows a group of Legionnaires coming towards our headquarters."

"How many?"

"It's just a handful, but they seem to be heavily armed."

"What do you think they are looking for?"

"My guess is that they are looking for their missing General." Vick says sarcastically.

"Well, there is no way they'll be able to climb the mountains if they are carrying a heavy load. Any idea how they plan on proceeding?"

"We know that they are following their General's path almost exactly. So, whatever he did, he left a nice clear trail."

Upon hearing those words, Violet is somewhat troubled. She had hoped that he would be dumb enough not to leave a trail, but it appears that he has a little more sense than that. Well, she has to give him some credit. Even though he's not book smart, he has some street sense.

"What kind of trail are they following?"

"From what I can tell, he basically made sure that he left evidence of where he was going, such as trampling the grass and leaving the remnants of campfires in clear view. He also made sure to stay on the highly traveled paths."

"Oh, so what you are telling me is they may not be following *his* trail, in particular, but *a* trail."

"Well, it's one and the same at this point."

"That may be true, but the implications are vastly different." Violet says as she rolls her eyes. Perhaps, Thom is not as smart as her men are trying to give him credit for.

"How far have they gotten?"

"They are half way up the mountain."

"I want to see your surveillance photos," Violet says as she extends her hand. Garrett pulls out a manila folder from the stack in front of him, and Violet opens it to reveal several photographs.

It looks like there are five people hot on his trail. They are all carrying at least two rifles each and a personal handgun at their side. From the looks of their belts and packs, they are also carrying thousands of rounds of ammunition. Guess that is to be expected. Thom *is* a very important officer in the Legion, and they probably want to find him as soon as possible.

Squinting, Violet tries to make out the faces of any of the men shown on the photographs, but cannot seem to recognize anyone. Even though it is pretty obvious that they are soldiers, they are not in uniform. It's as if the Legion headquarters does not want anyone to know who they are. That way, in the event that they are captured, they can deny being part of the Legion.

In addition, she notices that there are no obvious forms of communication on their bodies, which is quite odd for a mission such as this. Wouldn't they want to be able to contact headquarters if they come into contact with a large enemy force or if they face any obstacles?

Considering that they are heavily armed, this looks more like a suicide mission than a rescue one.

Even though Violet's intuition is almost always correct, these are just hunches. Right now, she needs to figure out who they are and stop them from completing their mission. Whatever it may be.

Holding the pictures up in the air, she announces, "Can anyone tell me who these people are in these pictures?" After being met with nothing but silence and shaking of their heads, she lets out a sigh and says, "I want names, people! Dismissed."

After everyone else leaves, Violet says to Trip, "Well, should we just go ahead and take them out?"

"No, I want to see how far they can go."

"Ugh, you are no fun. I take that to mean you want Lillian to capture them, too?"

"Yes."

"Understood."

*

After breakfast, Max takes Thom back to his room. He is pretty sure that Thom will get one of his own later, but the one that he is staying now is inadequate. Right now, the floor is not the most comfortable thing to be on. Feeling sorry for his injury, Max lets his friend take the bed even though he is the one with the scars to show for his session today.

Finally having a moment alone, Thom asks, "So, how are you holding up?"

"Oh, I'm doing fine," Max replies without looking him in the eye.

Now that he knows Max has lost both of his parents, he is not sure how to comfort him. No matter what he says, he feels that it would be insincere because he doesn't really understand what Max is going through right now. So much so that he feels a wedge has been placed between them. Throughout their entire lives, they have never had a problem telling one another the truth. They can say anything and know that the other will understand, even if it comes out wrong. But, this is different. Max absolutely loved his ...

Before he can finish his thought, Violet bursts into the room after a quick knock.

"I see you are still alive. Feeling better?" She says teasingly to Thom.

"Yes, no thanks to you," Thom says curtly.

"Oh, come on. If that's the worst thing anyone has ever done to you, you should count yourself lucky. Try getting shot three times in the chest."

After hearing her rebuttal, Thom does feel better. It really *is* a relative thing. He has never lost any limbs. All of his injuries have healed. And, he has never lost anything or anyone he really cared about. Even in the Legion, he has seen many casualties on the field, but he's never felt the grief of losing one close to him.

Once again, she interrupts his quiet contemplation and says, "I need you to tell me who are in these pictures."

Not knowing what to expect, Thom is not sure if he even wants to look at them. For all he knows, she might be showing him pictures of dead people his men have killed just to get a rise out of him. As he hesitantly takes a peek, he is relieved. He is glad to see that his men are coming to look for him.

"I see you know who they are," Violet says.

"Yes."

"Are you going to tell me or do you want to do this the hard way?"

"I think you already know who they are."

"We know that it's your rescue crew, but we need a little more detail than that."

"What difference does it make what their names are?"

"Come on, now, Thom. In times of war, any credible knowledge is power. You know that. That's why your father spreads lies about us, isn't it?"

Taking offense to the accusation, Thom says, "What are you saying about my father? How dare you?!"

Max is not sure he wants to be in this conversation. From what he has read in his mother's journal, he knows exactly what Violet is trying to say, but being Victor's son, Thom's reaction is perfectly understandable. Being his best friend, he really does not want to take the side against him, either.

As he tries to inch his way closer to the door, Violet says, "Max, would you care to tell your dear friend what your mother said in her journal about the rumors?"

Looking like he has just been stabbed in the heart, Thom gives Max an incredulous look, "Do you actually believe what she is saying about my father?"

"Please don't put me in the middle of this," Max begs.

"You are in this, like it or not," Violet says. "Who do you think killed your parents?"

"What?!" Thom shouts. "Now, you are accusing my father of killing Mr. and Mrs. Sullivan?"

*

Come on, Max, you can do it. Violet looks at Max, trying to convey her thoughts to him. You know in your heart that it's true. Even if he isn't the one who actually slit their throats, Victor is the one responsible for your parents' death. The only way that Thom is going to come to our side is if you convince him of his father's guilt.

Violet is getting tired of this long, dragged out war. She is convinced that Thom is the key to end it all. If Max can persuade him, it would make this go by so much faster, but if he cannot, at least the idea has been put in his mind. He will have no choice but to think about the possibility. Eventually, he will have to come to terms with the truth.

Unlike Victor who has no problem burning down everything, Trip refuses to hurt innocent bystanders. Because of his kindness, he has been reluctant to take out the Legion with an all-out battle. To some of those in the underground, however, his hesitation is seen as weakness. Ironically, because they fear El Diablo's wrath, they never say it out loud.

*

After pausing for a moment, Max looks Thom in the eyes and says, "I don't know what to believe any more. But Violet does have a point. My mother was highly suspicious of your father. There was good reason why my parents stopped working for the Legion."

Looking betrayed, Thom says, "I don't believe you! What have they done to make you think that, Max, after all that my family has done for you? How could you?!"

Despite his denial, a part of him knows that Violet and Max are telling the truth. But, without undeniable proof, he refuses to admit it. After all, did Mrs. Sullivan actually *say* that his father was guilty of anything? No! True, she has thrown around a lot of hints and innuendos, nothing more. Then again, he has never heard her criticize or accuse anyone out right of any wrongdoing even if it is true.

Come to think of it, he has never once asked the question – is my father is good man? Why would he? What kind of a child would ask a question like that? Especially about a father who has provided for him and tried to be there for him as much as possible.

Only an ungrateful and cynical fool would. But, now, he is forced to ask that dreadful question.

So, what does he know about his father? He is an elusive man, even to his own family. He is distant, not because he wants to be, but because he feels a need to be in order to protect them. What he does in his office is a mystery, even to his second in command, his own son. Why is that? Or, is Thom really his second in command? If not, who is?

Is it General Hawk? Is that why he is the only one who seems more agreeable than the other officers? When he introduced Max to everyone, he was the only one who did not verbally complain about having a private in the meeting. Of course, Thom was too preoccupied to see if his body language said otherwise. He left Hawk in charge while he's gone. What is he going to do?

"Can I see those pictures again?" Thom asks.

Smiling, Violet knows this is a good sign.

After studying the images, Thom looks disappointed.

"What's the matter?" Max asks.

"Nothing," Thom replies flatly, hoping that he has not given away his thoughts.

"Oh, come on, Thom. I am an expert at reading people and you are screaming *trouble* over there," Violet says tauntingly.

If it were just Max in the room, he may have been willing to share his thoughts and feelings, but he still cannot speak his mind openly with Violet. But, the truth of the matter is she can easily guess and she is usually correct.

"Don't tell me. They are just the peons to look for you," Violet continues.

Thom is surprised at how good she is at reading him. He is starting to admire her. In the back of his mind, he is thinking that he can really use someone like her on his team. The question is which team is he on?

Patting him on the shoulder, Max says, "That's OK, Thom."

Feeling a little put down, Thom puts on his poker face and says, "I don't know what you are talking about. These are fine men."

"Who are they?" Violet asks, not believing a word he just said.

"They are the rescue team, of course."

"Really? You are going with that generic, condescending answer?"

"Fine! So what if I don't know who they are, specifically? Do you know the names of every member of your team? The fact that they came looking for me and are hot on the trail means that I am a well-respected member of the Legion. So, what of it?"

"Calm down! I guess I really pushed your buttons there. I am simply making a point here. All I am saying is that I personally think someone else is pulling the strings in the background and it's not your father. If he were, he would have sent a better rescue team and would have done so much earlier. Can you think of anyone in the Legion who has ill will against you?" Violet says with a serious face.

Thom has not thought about the possibility before, but she does have a point. His father would have never sent such a small team to look for him, especially in such a difficult terrain where there may be hidden dangers everywhere. Whoever dispatched these men must have been doing it as a slight and could care less if these men, or him for that matter, come back alive or not.

In fact, there is a possibility that the mastermind behind this little rescue debacle hopes the team does not return. Because then, he has an excuse to destroy the mountains using heavy artillery from afar and would not have to send any soldiers on foot. If Thom gets killed in the process, he can pretend to mourn while happily awaiting his promotion.

So, who stands to gain by his demise? There are so many to choose from. In fact, any of his high ranking officers can be included. Being only eighteen years old, Thom is the youngest among them all and never saw a reason to train a successor or protégé. In other words, there is no one that he trusts to take over his position. With him out of the way, any of them can vie for the highly coveted job. The only condition is that whoever succeeds him would have to win his father's favor.

Next question, who despises him the most? This may be a difficult question to answer. Thom has always been quite oblivious about this sort of thing. Once again, his age has something to do with it. Being the youngest, he is used to jealousy and gossip. He is well aware of the fact that most of the officers talk behind his back, mocking him for being daddy's little boy. Hence, he never pays attention to any of them.

As he continues to ponder, his reservation about his team shows clearly on his troubled face. Satisfied that she has put enough doubt in his mind, Violet says, "I will leave you two alone now."

Max, in the meantime, is not sure what to think. Although he does not know Thom's men well, he believes Violet has a very valid point.

"Do you want to talk about it?" Max asks Thom after Violet leaves.

Forcing a smile, Thom says, "What is there to talk about?"

Max knows that his friend is torn but is not willing to share his disturbed thoughts right now. Max can tell that what Thom needs is time, so he will give him all the time he needs.

"Want to go for a walk?" Max asks.

Smiling again, Thom nods.

Chapter 12: The Rescue

"What is the status?" Victor says in a calm voice without moving from his leather bound chair.

"We have picked up his trail, Sir!" Lieutenant Gillnet replies.

Being the head of intelligence, he knows that it's his job to locate Thom as soon as possible. He also knows that Victor is neither a patient nor predictable man. There is no telling what he'll do if he gets angry.

There have been officers who have simply disappeared into thin air in the middle of the night. No one ever dared to ask or try to find the missing men. They all know what happened to them.

On the positive side, when something like that happens, most of the other officers are not all that surprised. Victor does not usually react solely based on emotion. There are reasons for his commands. While not everyone may agree with what those reasons are, there is nonetheless a valid one, at least in his mind.

"Where is he?" Victor continues his line of questioning.

For a man who just found out that his only son, the one he has been grooming since birth, is missing, he is actually quite at ease. What Gillnet is worried about is that despite the peaceful external expression he is currently wearing, he knows Victor is boiling on the inside and is ready to erupt at any time. Like Mount Vesuvius lying dormant, he can give you a sense of false assurance and destroy everything in his path if he thinks the time is right.

"We believe the rebels have captured him, Sir!"

"How did that happen?"

"He informed us of his plan for a vacation in the mountains about a week ago and gave us specific instructions not to follow him. It wasn't until several days later when we realized that he went off the grid, Sir!"

"And who should I thank for this indiscretion?"

Sweat pours down Gillnet's face. He knows that Victor is not happy with the turn of events and that he is to blame. He certainly does not intend on being one of the *statistics*. After all of the hard work that he has put in over the last decade, he is hoping that Victor will be lenient towards him.

"Sir, we followed his orders to the letter."

"So, if his instructions are for everyone to get in front of the firing squad, are you going to be the first one in line?"

His heart is pounding faster than ever before, even faster than when he'd been in the midst of battle. Victor's rhetorical question is impossible to answer. If he says yes, he may actually wind up in front of the firing squad. If he says no, he is being insubordinate. It's a lose-lose situation no matter what. All he can do is look at the floor.

"What's the matter? Are you going deaf or mute?"

Again, another unanswerable question. Gillnet knows he is in horrendously deep water and there's no rescue boat anywhere to be seen. The only thing he can do is redirect and hope that Victor is not going to call him on it.

"Sir, we have deployed five of our best men and we are hot on his trail."

"So, you think five men can take out the entire rebel camp, huh? I applaud your confidence. When can we expect his return?"

Ah! Another one! Victor is full of impossible questions. Gillnet is starting to get a flash back from his youth. Because of pressure from his parents to be at the top of his class, he often had nightmares where he forgot to study for a test and everything on the paper made no sense to him. In his dreams, the questions were literally illegible. There were strange symbols that look like hieroglyphics, but were not. Even though he understands what is going on, his level of anxiety is increasing at an alarming rate.

Even though he has a pretty good idea that Thom is in the mountains, it is a vastly large and unforgiving terrain. Based on recent sightings, the rebels are most probably in it, which makes the rescue mission that much more difficult. There is no telling if they have snipers who will pick them off one at a time or if they have set traps that will lead any intruders to fall to their deaths.

But, what should he say to Victor Richardson, the Generalissimo of the Legion? While few men have the privilege to know his official rank and title, no one dares to go against him. It's an unspoken understanding that all men in the Legion headquarters have. If they need to address anyone, they would call for Thom. If they need anything done, they know Victor is the man to go to, but it's impossible to go to him for a private audience without a referral.

They would need to have the ears of one of the high ranking officers in Thom's inner circle first. Of course, the price for gaining Victor's ear is steep – and for good reason. If Victor does not like what he hears, the messenger in the middle can get in hot water very quickly. As Gillnet is feeling right now, there is no escape once Victor becomes agitated.

On the other hand, the lucrative income is highly attractive. For those who have never felt Victor's wrath or think that the rumors are highly exaggerated, they are more than willing to take the risk.

Unfortunately, a phenomenon started to happen among the ranks. Bribery quickly led to corruption. When the officers who were not enticed originally saw the newfound riches that their less than honorable colleagues were getting, jealousy and peer pressure led them to follow suit.

Before long, just about every member of the high-ranking officers in the Legion had been bought at one time or another during their tenure.

The only officer who does not seem to be in on such schemes is Thom, for three very good reasons. First, being Victor's son, they are not sure how he would take it. It's possible that he will run to his father and tell him about what is going on and everyone would be shot.

Second, Thom is already rich. Having had everything handed to him his entire life, from a material stand point anyways, he has no need for more money. If he wants anything, he can just buy it or his parents will do it for him. Hence, he has never cared to increase his financial empire.

Third, Thom is a very loyal and honest man. While there are other men who also have principles, he has a much stronger will. He would have been angered by such propositions. Once again, he would probably tell his father and that would be the end.

Being as shrewd as he is, Victor knows everything that is going on, but like the episode in Algoma, he does not really care unless it gets in the way of his business. Yes, technically, his men are his business, but he decides to turn a blind eye to it, at least publicly. He figures as long as they are obedient to him and do their jobs as he commands, he doesn't care. That's good enough for him.

It's like his parenting skills, really. As long as Thom loves him or thinks he does, he is happy just showering him with possessions rather than affection. It's not that he does not know that Thom needs to be loved. It's that he thinks it's a mere detail if he appears to be happy. And, Victor's happiness is the only goal that Gillnet has right now.

Snap, snap! Victor says, "Am I boring you?"

"No, Sir! I am sorry, Sir!"

Whatever comes out of Gillnet's mouth next needs to be worded perfectly if he hopes to have a long life. He knows that he will be accountable for whatever answer that he provides. If the answer is too short, he will most likely fail. If the answer is too long, Victor will let him have it.

"In three days, Sir!" Gillnet decides to blurt out. He has no idea if that is sufficient or not, but that is the best he can come up with right now.

"Dismissed." Victor says flatly.

Walking out of the conference room, Gillnet can finally take a deep breath. He has exactly 72 hours to bring Thom back or his neck is on the line. He is terrified that he may lose something valuable. He couldn't imagine just what he would lose if Thom is not returned in time or has so much as a scratch on him when he does.

Before his meeting with Victor, he was actually glad that Thom was not here. He is tired of the pompous attitude of that eighteen-year-old. It seems that every time he sees that immature adolescent, he is prancing around like a spoiled child rather than acting the way that a general should be, poised and refined, like himself. He has always hated that boy because he never thought for one second that he deserved his position. He could care less if he fell off a bridge and was never seen again.

He only sent those five men to look for him because of pure curiosity. He had wanted to spy on him, but managed to lose track of him. When he dispatched the men, he had no intention of actually bringing him back. He was actually hoping that he would fall and injure himself. That way his much coveted position in the Legion would be open for someone more deserving, like himself. Now, he has no choice and no time left to complain.

He quickly sends out an emergency meeting request in hopes of gathering all of the officers together to brainstorm a strategy. Being merely a lieutenant, however, he has difficulty getting many of the higher ranking ones to show up.

Instead of attending, Major Fouke sends a private to deliver a note which simply states, "Busy, cannot participate. – F."

Seething with anger, Gillnet balls up the paper and throws it in the trash bin. "How dare him! Tell him if he does not show up, he will have to answer to the Generalissimo."

The private looks up in terror. Nobody ever dares to drop the generalissimo's name, or title for that matter. Doing so without cause would definitely get him in trouble. This must be a very serious meeting. All those who have shown up for the meeting are beginning to think so, too.

"Yes, Sir!" the private replies and runs off to tell his superior.

Within minutes, Fouke is at the door and says, "What is so important that you need to drag me out of bed?"

It's 2PM and hardly bed time. Judging from his appearance, Fouke does not appear to have been sleeping, either, but Gillnet gets the message. No matter if he is busy or not, Fouke is not about to do anything for him.

Standing at the head of the table, Gillnet is sweating profusely by now. "Gentleman, I know you are all very busy," he says without skipping a beat, "but we have an emergency on our hands."

"What exactly is this little emergency of yours? Are you not able to find your favorite caviar in the black market?" Fouke says with his usual sarcasm.

Already angered by his previous show of disrespect, Gillnet tries as hard as he can to ignore him and continues, "We have good reason to believe that our beloved General Thom Richardson has been kidnapped."

Beloved? At the sound of that word, he has grabbed the attention of all of the officers present. Gillnet of all people would have never described Thom as *beloved*. He obviously had a run in with Victor and is afraid to use any other adjective to describe his son.

"We have less than 72 hours to retrieve him." Gillnet says. "And, I need you all to team together and come up with a plan."

"Why should we? If that brat disappears, that's less trouble for us, right?" Fouke remarks while everyone else simply sits there with their arms crossed.

Even though none of them are a big fan of Thom's, they all know better than to refer to him as a brat in public. Who knows if that is going to get back to Victor? It's safer and definitely smarter to not say anything at all about it.

Ignoring him completely, Gillnet is starting to wonder if this meeting would proceed much faster without Fouke present. Oh, well, it's too late to ask that question now. He takes out the reports that his team had given him for the last few days and starts to show everyone where he believes Thom has been and where they lost all sign of him.

Everyone else becomes solemn as they listen to the seriousness in his tone. They all lean in to look at the map that he has put on the table and begin to ask questions about the mountain and what Gillnet's intelligence officers have found out about the region itself. Before long, General

Hawk has agreed to lead fifty able-bodied men to scour Thom's last known location.

*

Knock, knock. "What is it?" Violet says through the door.

Vick opens the door and says, "Sorry to interrupt. We just received word that the Legionnaires are approaching."

"How many?"

"About fifty of them."

"What's the prognosis?"

"They don't appear to be heavily armed. We believe it's a rescue mission."

"Haha! They finally sent a decent sized team to rescue Thom. How adorable! Well, what kind of hosts are we if we don't send out a welcome party, huh? You know what to do."

"Yup. Things are already in motion."

This is the moment of truth. Now that both Max and Thom are beginning to come over to their side, at least from a psychological standpoint, the question is how they are going to react to the news. The first wave of the rescue team is nothing more than a joke. The second wave is a much better effort.

Considering that the first wave is still in the mountains, however, Violet deduces that these two teams were dispatched by different people. Because of the spirit in which the first team was sent, they probably have no idea that there is another group following them. And, the second team has no intention of telling them, either. If they get caught in the middle, they'll be considered collateral damage.

With this new development, Violet decides to give the first team a few clues so they can be captured faster for both their own protection and for simplifying things. Assuming that they lack the experience to spot a trap, she heads to the mountains and starts creating a complex, yet obvious trail that leads right to the same exact place where Thom was captured.

To seal the deal, she takes the materials that Thom originally had and plants them in plain view, so it seems like an ideal place for them to search.

It doesn't take long before they catch sight of the trail and up their speed in order to make it there.

They walk right into their trap, with Lillian and Adam capturing them soon after.

*

After walking through Trip's garden, Thom feels better – not about the situation, but about himself. Even though he is still angered by the rag tag team that the Legion sent to rescue him, he is starting to see things clearer now. Instead of feeling sorry for himself, he is more determined than ever to be the leader of the military.

The difference between now and back then, however, is that he is going to pay more attention to the people themselves rather than the strategy. Instead of blindly carrying out orders from his father, he is going to find out why the orders have been given. After reading Mrs. Sullivan's journal, he is sure that many of the orders he carried out were probably based on hearsay and many innocent people may have been killed because of it.

So, the first person he wants to investigate is Mrs. Sullivan's former boss, Lieutenant Gillnet.

As he and Max begin to make their way out of the garden, a familiar figure appears on the horizon.

"There you two are!" Violet says. "I have been looking everywhere for you."

"Hope you didn't think we escaped," Thom says casually.

"I am so glad you are back to your usual self!" Violet says as she pats him on the back. "Come on. I have something to show you. Hope you are prepared."

"Prepared for what?" Thom asks suspiciously.

"Oh, you will see."

As they all walk back towards the building, she opens the door to one of the many rooms in the all too familiar hallway. Neither Max nor Thom knows what to expect.

A part of Thom suspects that she is going to introduce them to someone else. Then again, since he has already met El Diablo and the Warrior, who else can he possibly need to be prepared to meet?

After entering the room, Thom recognizes exactly where he is – the opposite of the room where he was kept when they first brought him into the compound. Just like that room, there is a large table with several chairs around it. The major difference is that he can see through this mirror, and there is no security camera in this room. Thom is somewhat surprised that he is now on this side of the mirror.

Do they trust him that much already? Or is this yet another test?

As he looks through the mirror, he is initially unsure of whom they are. Besides one confident man who is casually leaning against the wall, everyone else looks like any other man off the street, dirty, tired, and not exactly the most physically fit. Within seconds, however, he makes the connection. These are the five men who are in the rescue team, and Violet apparently wants him to watch the interrogation. They are all handcuffed to each other and to the table.

Thom finds it strange that all five men are in the same interrogation room at the same time. Isn't it customary to grill prisoners one at a time so they can find the truth and catch the ones who lie? Perhaps, the captors have so little respect for them that they expect them to tell them the truth immediately. Judging from the terrified looks on their faces, Thom's hunch may be right.

They looked a lot more courageous in the photographs than in person. Looking at these men, it seems that a part of them almost looks relieved to have been captured. Now, they no longer have to do the arduous work of climbing the mountains with their heavy gear and finally get the chance to sit down.

The other part of them looks understandably scared. These men don't look like they have ever been captured or even seen a day of battle in their lives. Some of them are scarily pale, like they have not even been outside of a building for months. Perhaps, they are administrative staff who are usually stuck in their small broom closets that they call offices in the Legion headquarters. Or, perhaps they are new trainees being put to a cruel test.

"I take it you are not impressed with this lot. Do any of them look familiar at all?" Violet asks, trying to give him the benefit of the doubt even though she already knows the answer.

"Nope, that makes the two of us."

Violet leans in and taps the small mic on the table before saying, "Okay, go ahead and start now."

The man across the mirror gives a quick nod.

Max takes a closer look and realizes that he recognizes the man doing the interrogation. It's Jordan, the man he used to talk with in the underground. He always thought of him as a friend. He had no idea that he would meet him in the Desiderios' headquarters, let alone in the interrogation room. He must be someone special.

Wait, does that mean Jordan was already spying on him way back when they spoke so candidly with one another? During the time he spent in the underground hideout making bombs, everyone was very uptight. Jordan was the only one who was relaxed and friendly.

Now that he thinks of it, was he really genuine or was he faking it just to get close to him? Max is certainly hoping it's the former. Besides Thom, he can hardly call anyone else a friend and he wants him to be one.

Jordan interrupts Max's thought as he starts off his questions. He puts both of his hands on the table as he leans into the face of the prisoner to the far right and says, "What's your name, son?"

"N-N-Nick, Sir," says the first terrified man.

"Nick, is it? Why don't you start off and tell us what you were doing in my mountain? And, you need to speak up, son. I am not as young as I used to be." Jordan asks as he gets so close to his face he could probably smell his breakfast.

Besides coffee, he seems to have had some bacon and sausage.

At twenty-five years of age, Jordan is hardly that much older than the other men in the room, but he certainly exudes a much more experienced vibe than any of them.

"We were on a mission, Sir."

"OK, I don't have all day. You are going to have to give more details quickly or I am going to get angry and you definitely don't want to see me get angry at you. I guarantee you will regret it."

"Yes, Sir. We left our posts three days ago and were told to find General Thomas in the mountains."

"Where is your post?"

Nick hesitates a second before he continues and says, "In the Legion headquarters about five miles north of here."

"You were stationed *in* the headquarters? What are your normal jobs?"

"I am a clerk, Sir. Cameron here is a translator. Jacob is a mechanic. Steven works in the kitchens, and Russell over there is new. He just joined us about a week ago. He is still in training, Sir."

Even though Thom had expected these men to be inexperienced, he is in shock to hear just exactly how inexperienced they really are for the mission that they were given.

"How are you planning on finding your general?"

"We have a picture of him, Sir," Cameron replies.

"Are you telling me you have never even met the man in person and have no idea what he looks like besides the picture?"

"That's correct, Sir," Nick continues.

"That photograph only tells you what he looks like. How do you know where to find him?"

"We were told to climb the mountain and just look for any signs of him."

"And what have you done to *just look*?"

"We figure since he is on vacation, he is not trying to cover his tracks. So, we followed the most commonly used paths along the mountain. Then, we saw evidence of someone dwelling near an overhanging just a bit off the path and decided to follow it."

Violet chuckles when she hears that her quick and sloppy plan to lure them into a trap worked like a charm. Of course, if these were trained soldiers on a serious mission, they would have figured out that the trail is too good to be true. She practical planted something obvious every twenty feet or so. It's almost like a scavenger hunt created for children.

"What happens if you meet enemy fire along the way? Do you even know how to use those heavy weapons that you were carrying?"

The men look at the floor until Russell, the trainee, raises his hand as if he is in grade school.

"Yes?" Jordan asks.

"I do, at least a little. I received some lessons during basic training Sir."

Rolling his eyes, Jordan says, "Anyone else? I am assuming that you were all trained when you first joined the Legion."

The other four men alternate looks from the floor to each other and finally to Jordan.

"Well?" Jordan asks impatiently.

"That is basically the extent of our training, Sir. After boot camp, we were assigned our tasks and have been doing them ever since. The only time we carry weapons is for drills. We don't ever fire our weapons."

Shaking his head, Jordan cannot believe what he is hearing. Then, he looks deep into each one of the men's eyes, one at a time, and asks the million dollar question that is in the minds of every one in attendance.

"Who sent you?"

All eyes are on the five frightened men as they anxiously await the answer. After they stare at each other for a few seconds, Jacob reveals Gillnet as the culprit behind this conniving scheme.

"There is that name again," Thom thinks to himself. He has heard enough. He is absolutely infuriated with the Legion and all of the backstabbing idiots who are supposed to work for him. In a huff, he is about to walk out of the room.

"Hold on, there. Where do you think you are going?" Violet asks.

"Anywhere but here," Thom says flatly.

"I cannot have you running around the rebel headquarters in an angry state. I am not saying this because I don't trust you. I am telling you this because if you do anything stupid, you are bound to get shot by one of my men."

"I won't. I am not dumb nor incompetent, contrary to what my former team mates think."

Violet almost feels sorry for the boy. She knows he is hurting very badly, not from the kind of pain that she has inflicted on him, but the type that is very difficult to heal. How do you recover from being ridiculed by your own men in such a defiant way? She looks over at Max who nods as he follows his best friend out of the door.

"Thom, wait! Please don't rush off," Max pleads with his best friend. "Let me help you."

"How do you plan on doing that?"

"Anything."

Even though Max's answer is really not an answer, Thom understands what he is trying to say. And, he is grateful for having such a good friend.

After calming down a little, he goes back to the room and sits down at the table to watch Jordan continue his little charade. Within minutes, he is no longer paying attention to what is going on in the other room. Instead, with each passing minute, he gets angrier at the Legion.

Different scenarios are going through his head. Even though Gillnet is the one who ordered these men to come, who else is in on it? How many men are plotting against him? Are there any that are plotting against his father? How much support does he still have with his men? How loyal are the soldiers?

Then, he looks at Max and asks himself: is he a part of the rebels now? If so, that means his father is the enemy. How can he pick sides between his father and his best friend? His gut tells him his friend is right but his heart wants to side with family. Is there another way? There seems to be no end to the questions and no way to decide.

Chapter 13: The Intruders

After the dog and pony show finally ends, Violet turns to Thom and says, "Ready for another kink in the chain?"

"Great... What else can go wrong now?" Thom asks.

"There is something else you need to know. Depending on how you take this news, it may be good or bad." Violet replies.

Violet proceeds to tell the two men about the second group of Legionnaires coming towards them. Instead of telling them about her own suspicions of what she thinks they may be, she wants to give them a chance to say what's on their minds first. Regardless of whether or not this is the real rescue team, the new intruders look much more menacing.

Once again, she asks, "Any idea who these people may be?"

After seeing the horrible display of disrespect from his men, he is not expecting anything positive and says, "Are they here to destroy you guys?"

"Take a look for yourself," Violet answers as she shows him a surveillance picture of the new intruders.

As he studies the grainy photograph, he looks to see if there is anyone in this new group that is more than a pencil pusher. To his surprise, he does. In fact, he recognizes many of the men. They seem to be actual soldiers who have fought alongside him on the battlefield once or twice before. Yet, from what he can see, each man is only carrying a backpack with harnesses.

Instinctively, he says with a serious face, "This is the *real* rescue team, isn't it?"

Then, Thom's eyes light up. For that split second, he regains the hope that his men *do* care for him and perhaps that first crew was merely the scouting team, not a rescue one. Then, reality sets in. He remembers the words of the five helpless men in the interrogation room. There is no mistake. Gillnet sent them to deliver a message and to make a point. He wants to make it perfectly clear that *he* is in control over at the Legion headquarters.

If that is the case, that means someone more powerful and commanding sent these men, despite Gillnet having already sent out a so-called rescue team. The only man he can think of with that amount of power is his father. If Victor is behind this team, the Desiderios will be on high alert. Unlike the previous group, this one certainly looks serious.

Once again, Violet can read his expression. "So, you think this will be a bloody battle?"

"I hope not, but I think it will be."

"Whose side will you be on?" Violet asks, eager to hear his response.

"I don't know," Thom replies as he sits back down and covers his head with his hands.

He didn't see his father in the picture. That means he is still at Legion headquarters. Why wouldn't he? His father has not been on the field since Thom took command of the soldiers. That is really the reason that he was promoted to the rank of General in the first place, to take his father's place on the ground without him having to relinquish any authority.

Thom argues that his father is too old to climb a mountain. Even if it is to save his only son, it would be too dangerous for a man of his age. He would not want Victor to get hurt looking for him. He would not be able to take that kind of guilt if something were to happen to him.

Besides, he has only been gone for a mere week. Most people's vacations do last that long. It's not like he has been missing for a month. So, there is really no need for anyone to panic yet. If he were in his father's shoes, the only reason he would have sent a 50-member team is out of an abundance of caution. After all, he did give specific instructions to leave him alone.

Nevertheless, regardless of how he reasons it, he still feels irritated by the way the Legionnaires have treated him. Right now, his main goal is to regain control of his men.

*

"Good morning, everyone, I have gathered you all here today because we have a potential crisis on our hands," Violet says.

By the look on Trip's face, everyone knows that she is dead serious. There is no way he would have attended an emergency meeting with such a serious look unless there is indeed a real threat.

"I believe all of you already know about the new group of intruders coming our way."

Several of the men nod.

"We have reason to believe that they are not just Legionnaires who are here to rescue Thom. Take a look at the live feed from the surveillance videos for yourself."

At the sound of those words, Violet has the Desiderios' full attention if she didn't already. In order for them to be seen live, the intruders must be very close to their headquarters, too close for comfort.

"The question that I am sure is on everyone's mind is: how did they get here so quickly? Has anyone seen or heard anything out of the ordinary lately or on your posts?" Violet asks as she stares at everyone in the room.

While some of the members shake their heads, others are looking at the screen. No one has anything to offer.

Then, Trip says, "I want updates on the underground activities."

Surprise spreads across the group as everyone stiffens at the sound of his voice. He usually observes and usually only for a few minutes before taking off. The fact that he's making direct commands means that this is more important than anything they'd done before.

Then, they all look at Jordan, the interrogator who is on an undercover mission at the hideout.

"There has been some unrest among the men," Jordan admits, "But nothing really out of the ordinary."

"Is there anyone who may be suspicious?" Violet asks as she continues to lead the meeting after Trip once again deigns to speak.

"No one that can be classified as suspicious but there are some whom I think should be watched."

"Do tell."

"Some of the bomb making squad has been quite daring lately. There have been a few times when they could have blown up the facility accidentally."

"Are these actual accidents or do you think they are doing it on purpose so they can tip off the Legionnaires?"

"I am beginning to wonder that myself. But, so far, none of them have been loud enough to raise any suspicion on the ground level. We are deep enough underground that it does not trigger any detection devices on the surface."

"Do any of them know where our headquarters are?"

"No."

"Are you absolutely positive?"

"Yes."

Judging from his expression, Violet is convinced that he is telling the truth, but she is also certain that there is a mole somewhere within the Desiderios. It is just too convenient. There is no way that the Legionnaires can pinpoint their location so accurately. This is a vast mountain to scour through and the path to the rebel headquarters is not an easy one.

There are two ways to reach it. The most well-known method that members of the Desiderios use requires them to know where to start first. There is no special landmark that identifies it, which is the beauty of the spot. Second, they need to scale thirty feet of rock. For those unfamiliar with the terrain, it can be a deadly endeavor. Then, they need to find the entrance which is hidden behind a large boulder.

Once they find it, there is a five foot thick steel wall that can only be accessed with a retinal as well as a fingerprint scan. The entire area is also heavily secured and armed. There are ten hidden cameras that show every angle of the entrance that are watched 24/7. Any intruder will be shot on the spot by any number of the weapons concealed in the area.

Once they are cleared, they need to go through about a mile's worth of tunnel before reaching the rebel headquarters on the other side of the mountains. This way, if anyone forces their way in, it gives the rebels enough time to exit through the second way, which is an escape route. Only the highest ranking members of the rebels like Trip and Violet know it. So far, they have yet to have a reason to use it.

Because the path must be kept a secret, captured prisoners are always unconscious or blindfolded before they are transported inside. Even if the enemy tries to find the

212

location from the air, they would not be able to pinpoint the exact location because of the natural terrain with its twists and turns as well as the thick cover of the clouds.

Yet, the intruders have bypassed the well-traveled paths that Thom and the inexperienced rescue team had taken. Instead, they are already scaling the side of the mountain. Judging from the speed that they are climbing, they seem to know it well, as if they are being led by someone.

"OK, time is wasting. Team Delta, Team Beta, Team Gamma, you know what to do. Dismissed!" Violet shouts. "Not so fast, Jordan. Stay here."

Even though Violet's little post script to ask Jordan to stay piques the interest of some of the men, they let go of their curiosity immediately and disperse to go to their battle stations.

Wolfe is gathering Team Delta to prep the animals, the first line of defense. With the mountainous terrain, the easiest way to deter intruders is with large and ferocious animals. They have trained predators like bears, bobcats, mountain lions, and cougars to attack anyone they do not recognize. They also have some highly poisonous slithering reptiles, such as the infamous vipers, cobras, rattlesnakes, and copperheads. They even have attackers from the air, like hawks and falcons. Like his men, all of the critters are strong and highly trained.

Fisher is leading Team Beta. True to his name, he is patiently setting up the bait and awaiting his catch. The traps have been set up and lying in wait just for such an occasion. If the intruders manage to survive Wolfe's team, there are hundreds of booby traps using nature itself, ranging from loose rocks to spring loaded branches. For those who manage to avoid them, his men are ready to attack the soldiers from positions hidden from the naked eye. All of those in Team Beta have been trained to be deadly silent and fast.

213

Garret is heading up Team Gamma, the ones guarding the entrances. If the intruders survive the first two teams, Garret's team is ready to shoot anyone on sight. He has some of the best sharpshooters that anyone has ever seen on his team.

Because most of the rebels have seen the destruction that the Legionnaires are capable of, they train longer and harder than anyone else. In turn, they are stronger, faster, and more accurate than their enemies.

As for Jordan, he knows why he is staying. After hearing Violet's line of questioning, he knows that either Violet or Trip suspect that he may be the mole. After all, he is the only one of the regulars in the underground hideout that knows the location of the headquarters. Based on the low amount of people that know about the entrance, and the fact that the enemy so easily knows the route, it's easy to see how they would put two and two together.

He is used to being on the other side of the interrogation, but he knows when to keep his cool. And that time is definitely now. If he appears to be nervous, Violet will be able to see right through him and corner him with her constant barrage of questions. Once he gets in that situation, it would be very difficult for him to defend himself, leading him to look guilty.

"Look, it's not me," Jordan says.

"What's not you?" Violet asks, pretending to not know what he is talking about.

"I know you think I am the mole, but I am not," Jordan says flat out.

"What makes you say that?"

So, the game has begun. The best way to win this is to be straight with her and get to the point as soon as possible. The longer the conversation drags on, the more likely it is for him to lose. Being an interrogator himself, he knows exactly what she is going to do. More than likely, she is going to use intimidating tactics and try to corner him until he folds. By having Trip over there for effect, she can really drive her point home. But, he is not going to let that happen.

"Because both of you have been eyeing me since we started the meeting and Trip never does that unless there is a very good reason," Jordan says without skipping a beat.

Violet raises an eyebrow, impressed that he had noticed that. The truth of the matter is, she assigned him to the underground precisely because he pays attention to details.

"OK, then, give us a reason to believe you, besides your words."

"I am not going to bore you with tales of my loyalty. If you don't know them already, there is no point telling it to you now."

"Good point. What else?" Violet says as she crosses her arms.

After knowing Jordan for the last eight years, she has never seen him do anything disloyal, which, of course, is not the same as being completely loyal. As far as she knows, he has always performed his job well, reported anything suspicious, and kept her in the loop of all of the projects that are going on in the hideout. So, there is really no reason to doubt him, but she needs to know who may be the culprit if not him. Right now, he is the only plausible suspect that she has.

"The only thing I can do is help find the real mole."

"OK, tell us something that we can use."

Jordan studies the live feed, searching for any familiar faces. "I have a strong feeling that the mole is among those men somewhere. To hide his identity, he will not be in the front or the rear. He will be mixed among the soldiers somewhere inconspicuous. He will also not do anything to draw attention to himself. So, it will be a little difficult to spot. But, it should be someone that I have seen before in the hideout, if your hunch is correct. This person would have either followed me or tracked my route somehow during my trips to the headquarters. That would be the only way that he knows how to get here. Because I am usually very careful about checking my surroundings, this person must be very good at what he does."

Good Point. Violet silently agrees with his explanation. He has done a fairly good job of profiling the perpetrator. Since Jordan is the only one who knows the people working in the hideout, she really has to trust his instincts and knowledge of the people there.

After watching him stare at the video for a few minutes, she says, "Well? Anything?"

"No, not yet. I wish these videos were clearer. Every time I think I see someone I recognize, I don't know for sure because they are all dressed alike. From this angle, it's almost impossible to identify them."

"What are you saying? Is it time for a field trip?"

"Perhaps."

Trip is already out the door. Seeing that time is of the essence, Violet grabs Jordan's shoulder and follows their fearless leader without uttering a sound.

As the three of them exit out the large steel door, they go to the right corner of the cliff where there are several large boulders. In between two of them is a small hideout already containing a man holding a sniper gun, likely from Team Gamma, that gives a perfect view of the men climbing up the mountain without being seen.

*

For a minute, Thom ponders whether or not he should warn the intruders. Since they are technically *his* men, he certainly does not want to see them get slaughtered. But, then again, he does not know the true intentions of the second team. Even though he believes his father sent them, he may be wrong.

There is a possibility that they may not be on a rescue mission, but instead, they're on a mission to kill him. These are well trained soldiers who are fighters, not rescuers. In fact, he doesn't think any of them has even been trained on how to conduct a rescue. If he recalls correctly, some of these men are fiercely loyal to Gillnet.

Also, he knows that the rebels, Violet and Trip in particular, can take him out within a second if he even dares to try. He has seen Violet in action and he knows he will lose in this situation. She is definitely wittier and faster than he is, and Trip does not look like the kind who will tolerate any scheming.

On the other hand, it may be worth the risk. If they wanted to kill him, they would have done so a long time ago. They are obviously keeping him alive for a reason. Unlike Max who seems to be a part of them already, he is still on the fence about how he should proceed. Even though he knows that there are obvious issues with the Legionnaires, he cannot just turn his back on them.

Although neither he nor Max were allowed to go to the meeting and do not know the details of their plans, he knows that something is up. Since this is rebel territory, there is no telling what kind of danger they are facing. Right now, he is stuck sitting in Max's room with him and there is no way for him to tell what the current situation is without snooping.

"What are you thinking of doing?" Max asks.

Thom starts at the sound of Max's voice. He'd almost forgotten that, just like Violet who can read Trip's mind, Max can do the same for him.

"I don't know. What would you do in my situation?" Thom asks. Since Max has always been the smarter one of the pair, he genuinely wants to know what he has to say.

Thinking logically, Max says, "The first thing you need to do is find out who these people are."

Needing Max's honest opinion, Thom is not afraid of being truthful to him at this point and says, "They are soldiers."

"Can you trust them?"

"That's the million dollar question, isn't it?" Thom says rhetorically before answering, "I don't know."

"Well, the thing about trust is if you don't know, the answer is usually a no, plain and simple. If you trust someone, you shouldn't have any doubts at all."

"That's a good point." The only reason he is as open as he is right now is because he completely trusts Max no matter what.

"If you don't trust them, I don't think you should risk your life for them."

"But what if I am wrong? What if they are here to rescue me?"

"Is there any man in that photograph whom you can trust?

Staring at the faces, Thom is disappointed to say that the answer is no. Perhaps that is also his fault. He has never really paid attention to any of the soldiers, either.

Ironically, his charismatic personality means that everyone respects him, but he is not close to anyone in particular. A small part of him is afraid that if they get too close, they may not like him as much as he wants them to.

"Well, since you cannot trust any of them, I think the best thing to do now is to ask them."

"That's definitely harder than it sounds. How do you propose we do that?"

"We need to intercept these men before the rebels get to them."

"Suggestions?"

"First, we need to find ourselves a change of clothes. We need to blend in with the rebels so we can get past the gates."

Nodding in agreement, the two men walk down the hallway casually to not arouse any suspicion as Max leads them to the laundry room. Thankful that there is a freshly cleaned batch already in the dryer, they each take out a set of uniforms, if you can call it that, and put them on. Unlike the Legionnaires, the rebels don't really have uniforms, per se, but they do wear the same dull color when they are in battle, so as to make sure that they'll be able to hide from enemies.

As they head out of the laundry room, Max does his best to lead Thom towards the tunnels that lead to the outside. He'd spent several hours exploring the darkest corners of the headquarters for this purpose only. You never know when you might need an escape route.

But as they attempt to appear casual walking through the tunnels, the hairs on the back of his neck stand up. He is sure that they are being watched and expects to be stopped at any minute.

Just as he suspects, Garret's team notices them trying to exit.

"Violet, we have a problem here."

"Talk to me," Violet says quietly, but impatiently.

"The young general and his buddy are heading your way in really bad disguises."

"Are they armed?"

"No. Should we stop them?"

Chucking, she says, "No, I want to know what they are planning on doing. Track them."

"Copy that."

As Thom and Max walk by, Garret motions for one of his men to stop them. As they're sweating it out with the guy's questions about where they are going, Garret pats them both on the back.

With that pat, he sticks on them a microscopic device which would allow them to hear their conversations and track their movements.

Garret leans over at his man and says, "Hey. I think we can let these two boys off for now, go report to your team, kids."

He pushes them off toward the exit with a smile on his face. They are horrible at disguises. They're supposed to have an insignia on their right arm stating what rank and team they are. Looks like they completely forgot about that when they were trying to disguise themselves.

Meanwhile, Trip turns to look at Violet, awaiting an update without saying a single word.

"Things just got a little more interesting," Violet whispers. "Thom and Max are heading this way."

From where they are hiding, they can get a pretty good view of the entrance to the headquarters, too. So, if the duo manages to find their way out, the rebel leaders can monitor their activity easily both visually and audibly.

Looking through the binoculars, Jordan is studying the faces of everyone he sees, one at a time. He knows that he needs to identify someone so he can get the spotlight off of *his* face. At the same time, he knows that Violet and Trip will be able tell if he is bluffing. So, he has to find someone for real and not just any random person who may look shady.

Hearing Violet's update about Thom, however, Jordan is not sure if that is going to be good or bad news for him. On one hand, he may be short on time. In the event that Thom reveals their location and blows their cover to the intruders, he may not have enough time to identify a suspect, which would make him look incompetent. And, it would not remove the focus from him.

On the other hand, if Thom is able to find the culprit, he'll be off the hook. After all, Trip only *suspects* that the mole is from the underground. If Thom can come up with another person of interest, he won't be on the spot anymore. Of course, even he knows that this is the less likely scenario. Trip and Violet are almost never wrong. After coming to that conclusion, he resumes his frantic search.

*

"How long is this tunnel?" Thom says impatiently as he rolls his eyes.

He is getting tired of walking through this long corridor with no end in sight. The only good thing he can say is that it is relatively dry and well lit. So, he isn't completely annoyed yet. Most of the tunnels that he has seen are usually damp, dark, and often filled with less than desirable rodents or pests.

Max doesn't say anything, too busy looking around the tunnel. He is sure that they have been made already. He is somewhat surprised that nobody stopped him. Of course, he has a strong suspicion that the rebels are watching their every move. Because the bug is so small, however, even Max is not aware that there is a tracking device already planted on them.

He shrugs off the worry for the moment and sighs inwardly at his complaining friend.

Thom is such a child sometimes. Instead of worrying about what he may face outside of this tunnel, he is whining about how long it is taking. Max is not sure if that's a sign of bravery or stupidity. In Thom's case, it's probably both.

Doesn't he realize that even though the rebels have not stopped them, there may be a very good reason? From what he has seen, every member of the Desiderios is pretty sharp. They never do anything without a good reason.

Like kidnapping the two of them. In this case, they may be waiting for Thom to give them a reason to shoot him. Or, perhaps they are waiting to see if the Legionnaires truly intend on rescuing him or if it's just a ruse to attack the Desiderios?

Regardless of the reason, Max knows that he needs to prep his friend before they exit the tunnel.

"Be patient. I am sure it's not too much longer," Max replies.

"You sure took a long time to answer that rhetorical question."

"Sorry, I was just thinking."

"About what?"

"How are you planning on picking the man to ask when you meet the rescue team?"

"Simple. I am just going to go up to them and ask."

"Isn't that a little risky?"

"Yes, but I *am* their general. The only man higher in rank in the Legion is my father. So, even if they have been given instructions to capture or kill me, I don't think they are going to carry it out because they know they will have to answer to my father if I turn up dead."

"That's a good point, but what if they blame the rebels for your death? Since he is not here with them, it's easy for them to lie if they need to."

"That's why you are here with me, my friend. If something happens to me, I want you to deliver the message to my father."

"What if we are both killed once we step outside?"

"That won't happen, because I want you to stay in the tunnel for a minute first. If you see any sign of danger, run back and inform El Diablo."

"You want me to run?"

Even though Max is not a fan of being in the military, running away when his friend may be in danger just seems too cowardly, even for a little guy like him.

"Yes, but you are not running *away*. You will be running to get help. That's two different things."

"Yeah, yeah. Po-tay-to, Po-ta-to."

Chuckling, Thom pats his friend on the shoulder and says, "I cannot let them hurt you, my little buddy!"

Max doesn't really know how he feels about that. A part of him is a little insulted that Thom still thinks he needs to be protected. The other part of him is very glad that he has a true friend.

Meanwhile, Violet smiles as she listens to their conversation. She can relate. She knows that Trip would do the same thing and try to protect her if they were in a similar situation. At the same time, she would never let Trip do it all by himself. That's just not what best friends do.

Chapter 14: The Truth

As Jordan scans faster, he stops back at a face and says, "There! That man! The tall one about a quarter way down with the blond hair!"

Trip and Violet both take out binoculars to take a look at the man he's talking about.

"Which blond one?" Violet asks with an exasperated sigh.

Jordan squints and tries not to lose him. "The one with the canteen. He's taking a drink of it now while the man on his right talks to him."

Violet and Trip both swivel at the same time as they locate the man in question.

"That man is a member of the underground."

"Are you certain?" Violet asks.

"Yes."

"Garret, do you copy?"

"Yes." Garret replies.

Being singled out as the mole, Violet wants to make sure that he is captured alive for interrogation.

"What's his stats?"

"I believe his name is Elliot. I have seen him in the underground before. He is on the bomb making squad, but he isn't one of the engineers who make the bombs. He is one of the supervisors. From what I know of him, he is not the nicest man. He is known to rough up some of the men if they don't do exactly what he tells them."

"Then, why is he still leading the squad?" Violet asks.

"Because he always delivers."

"That's no excuse. Such unacceptable behavior is going to lower the morale and turn our men against us. Why is this the first time I've heard of this man?"

"I am sorry. Since he has never seriously injured anyone, we thought it best to leave him in his position."

"Who's we?"

"The...other squadron leaders and I?" Jordan's response comes out more like a question than a statement, and he winces as he hears his own hesitation.

"So, this is a well-known problem and you just decide to ignore it?"

"I didn't want to burden you with such a trivial issue."

Both Jordan and Trip can tell that Violet is less than happy with the direction that this conversation is going. To stop herself from pushing Jordan off the cliff, Violet grits her teeth and makes a mental note to deal with him later. Right now, she needs to focus on the intruders.

Before long, they hear the first screams.

*

When the intruders are in the middle of their climb, one of Wolfe's mountain lions shows up seemingly out of nowhere as it walks purposely within feet of them with a menacing growl. As some of the men panic, they lose their grip, falling a few feet. Lucky for them, they are tied together with harnesses. Nevertheless, the men are rattled, shouting to each other as they try to escape the predator's grasp.

It's pretty obvious from Hawk's expression that he is more than a little irritated. His solders' outbursts are certainly loud enough to tip off the rebel forces which ruins the element of surprise. Even though he doesn't know it yet, it is really a moot point.

As one of the men takes out a handgun to try to shoot the animal, the mountain lion notices it and pounces on him. As he tries to avoid its deadly claws, he is knocked down several feet and loses his weapon in the process. Then, several more men take out their weapons and begin to fire. Being well trained, the agile animal dodges the majority of them while lunging at the men. Not all of them are as lucky as the first shooter. In their panic, some of the men detach their harnesses in hopes of escaping, which proves to be a fatal mistake as they lose their grip on the slippery mountain face and fall to the ground with a resounding thud.

In the midst of the confusion, Wolfe releases a viper near another group of soldiers. Unlike the mountain lion, this slithering soldier does not bother to wait. Instantly, it sinks its teeth into the first man it touches. Letting out a loud shriek, the man panics, sending those around him into a frenzy. One man who draws his weapon trying to shoot it ends up shooting one of his fellow men in the leg. Another man tries to snatch the snake, but is also bitten.

Hawk grimaces at the unruly state his men are in. They have no idea how to deal with this type of attack. Despite the briefing that he had given them before they started climbing, not a single soldier seems to have remembered the most important rule: Stay Calm.

Being an experienced climber, Hawk decides that he will have to be the one to save his men. When he set out for this mission, he made sure that he mingled in with everyone else to avoid being picked out as the leader, which is one reason why even Thom didn't find him in the photograph. But now, he has little choice but to expose himself.

In an attempt to calm his men down, he whistles as loud as he can and shouts, "Listen up, everyone! You need to calm down and follow me!"

At first, he can hardly hear himself in the loud ruckus, but as the men around him begin to quiet down, a domino effect happens throughout the rest of the group. And, within minutes, the chaotic shouting lowers as they await their leader's command.

He points to the men lying on the ground, pale and shaking as poison spreads throughout their bodies. "Pick them up and move them away from the fray. Be more cautious. These are obviously not wild animals. They have been trained. Treat them like you would an overly large enemy, several men to one animal. And stay in your ranks. You are dignified soldiers of the Legion, not brawling teenagers."

His men listen attentively to him and follow his orders to the letter as they begin climbing up again.

Some of the men step up to care for the injured by putting extra harnesses on them to carry them away to the doctors at the bottom of the mountain. They know that they don't have a great deal of time to get the venom out.

*

"Ah, ha! There is the leader! He looks familiar. Where have I seen him before?" As expected, Hawk's shouting has attracted the rebels' attention, in particular, Violet's attention.

"That's General Hawk," Jordan replies. "He is basically General Thom Richardson's right hand man and second in command."

"Really? Is he loyal to Thom?"

"That I am not sure."

"Well, we need to find out, don't we?"

Then, Violet puts her hand on her ear piece and says, "Ready, Team Beta?"

"Yes, Ma'am!"

Having heard the command, Fisher's face lights up. He has been waiting to see some real action for a long time and is finally getting the chance. His team usually sets up the traps and leaves before the fighting starts. With the enemy at the rebel gates, this is the first time he actually has a chance to see his hard work in action and to test the nerves of his men.

Wolfe's team has rattled the enemy so much that Violet has already called for the second wave of attack after only starting this battle a few minutes ago.

Instantly, poison darts start flying through the air, very much like the old days when archers would fire a barrage of flaming arrows into the enemy line. As more intruders begin to fall, they drag down their colleagues who are attached to them. Ironically, the harnesses are meant to save them from falling, but are now doing the opposite.

Meanwhile, Violet, Trip, and Jordan are keeping an eagle eye out for Elliot to see what he plans on doing. Fisher knows that he is not to touch either him or Hawk for two reasons. First, they need to be kept alive so they can be interrogated. Second, the rebels like to see how their enemies react and handle such a situation, because their actions tell a great deal about them without needing to be asked.

For example, are they going to save themselves or their comrades? Are they going to deviate from what the rest of the team members are doing? Any form of deviation in time of confusion is usually a dead giveaway for revealing their true mission. During chaotic times, no one notices when one man goes off to do something else, such as going through a hidden path or planting traps or bombs.

In Elliot's case, he has already detached himself from the harness and is climbing up the mountain on his own, leaving everyone else behind. Meanwhile, Violet is impressed that Hawk is trying to pull his men up without caring whether or not he gets hit. He is out in the open, an easy target for anyone passing.

Elliot seems to notice this too because as he climbs up, he heads toward Hawk. Before anyone can do anything, he pulls out his dagger and stabs Hawk in the back.

Hawk cries out in pain before trying to twist around and see who stabbed him, but it takes a mere second for Elliot to cut his harness and push him off.

Hawk falls down the mountain like a rock. No one could survive that.

"He killed him!" Violet yells in shock. "Fisher, change of plans. Capture Elliot now!"

"Copy that."

In minutes, Fisher's men come out of a tunnel and lie directly on top of the intruders.

They wait until Elliot is right below them before dropping a net on top of him.

While he attempts to disentangle himself from the net, a couple of men haul him up, grappling with him.

Elliot pulls out his handgun and tries to shoot one of the rebels, but he is tackled before he can pull the trigger. The shot ricochets off the rock walls. He punches the man who tackled him and tries to throw him off. Another man comes to help and holds him down before Fisher pistol whips him and knocks him unconscious.

They haul him up and begin carrying him to the interrogation room.

Along the way, Thom and Max finally reach the end of the tunnel. They cannot believe what is waiting for them outside. Instead of snipers getting ready to shoot them or Legionnaires trying to rescue or capture them, they are hearing the hurling screams of men as they fall from the cliff.

Those who are still alive are desperately trying to get down from the mountain as fast as they can in an attempt to escape. It seems nobody has noticed that Hawk is dead, either.

Within the hour, the remaining Legionnaires are either dead or have fled. They have lost the battle.

*

Being the professional that he obviously is, there is nothing in Elliot's possession that gives the Desiderios any clue as to his treachery. There are no names, no locations, and no numbers of any kinds. Knowing that this will be a little more difficult than the five hapless men who were in this room earlier that day, Violet is doing the interrogation while Trip, Jordan, Thom, and Max watch in the other room.

When Max sees Elliot, he instantly recognizes him and shouts, "That's him!"

"That's whom?" Thom asks curiously.

Before answering, Max hesitates for a second. After all, the only way that he would know who he is referring to is if he has read his journal. Considering that Thom already read his mother's journal and had his own journal in his possession when he came, there is a good chance that he has read his as well.

"That's the jerk from the underground!" Max answers.

Max is somewhat relieved to see that Thom does not seem quite sure who the jerk is at first. That can mean one of two things. It either means he has not read the journal or that he has a bad memory. Knowing Thom, however, Max is pretty sure it's the latter. In either case, he figures everyone in the room already knows about his past anyways.

So, he takes the time to elaborate and tells him about the abuses that he has received from Elliot in the past.

Even though Thom does recall this particular incident in the journal, he had no idea the extent of the abuse that Max had suffered until now. He is getting more upset with each passing second, but he has to calm himself down so he can listen to the impending interrogation.

*

Instead of her usual calm and casual self, Violet is very serious this time.

She slaps him hard on the cheek, once, twice. Unlike Max, she is not about to wait for Elliot to wake up by himself. While she cannot believe what she has seen this man do, she also knows when she needs to get things done. Right now, her priority is to find out what exactly happened.

"Wake up!" Violet says as she continues to slap him.

"Huh?" Elliot stares around when he finally awakens.

When his eyes focus on the woman in front of him, he lets out a slight shudder. He knows exactly who she is – the Warrior. If she is the one interrogating him, he knows he is in deep water.

Playing dumb, he says, "Where am I?"

"You know very well where you are."

"Who are you?"

"Again, you know the answer to that, too. If you are going to keep playing that game, I have ways of making you cooperate."

"What do you want from me?"

"The truth. Now, start talking."

"What do you want to know? I am just a lowly private in the Legion."

Violet's face begins to turn red. So he's going to keep playing the game. She gives him a solid punch to his gut, and he bends over as far as he can in his constraints, groaning in pain.

She says, "First strike. Guess how many you get?"

From the look on her face, everyone knows that she is dead serious, but he is determined to hold his ground as he sits there with his face screwed up in pain but his mouth closed.

"I see you need more instructions than what I have given you. Why don't I go easy on you and start off with a simple question. What is your name?"

"Elliot."

"Elliot what?"

"Young."

"See, that wasn't so hard, was it? Now, how long have you been working with the Legion?"

"Six years." Elliot answers truthfully. Since he has already announced that he is a Legionnaire, he figures it makes little difference how long he has been with them, but he is wrong.

"Uh, huh. After six years, you are still a private. You are either a completely incompetent soldier or a really bad liar. Seeing how you handled yourself today, I would say that your nose should be growing, Pinocchio." Violet says sarcastically.

Darn! Elliot could kick himself for being so careless already.

"What is your real rank in the Legion?"

"Captain."

"So, *Captain*, what was your mission today?"

"To rescue General Thomson."

"Then, why did you kill Hawk?"

Thom lets out a quiet "What?" as he watches Elliot. "Hawk is dead?" Having just come out of the tunnel when the battle was already ending; neither he nor Max saw what happened to the late general.

Hesitating for a second, he replies, "He was a traitor."

"How so?"

"He was planning on killing General Thomas when we find him."

Thom is even more surprised to hear this as he lets out a louder, "What?! Hawk was going to kill me?"

Jordan looks at him and puts his finger on his mouth and softly says, "Shhhh".

Thom is not sure how to take this latest information. Of all of the men who report to him, Hawk is the last person he would expect who would want to kill him.

Leaning in closer to stare deep into his eyes, Violet says with a chilling voice, "How was he going to do that with 50 of his men watching?"

It was obvious she didn't believe him whatsoever.

"Answer me."

234

She grabs his right wrist before twisting it brutally until a loud SNAP! is heard. He screams, shaking in his chair as he tries in vain to distance himself from her.

Max flinches when he hears Elliot's wrist break. Thom gives him a concerned look and smiles reassuringly at him.

Violet stays where she is, her hand on his injured wrist, her threat clear. Without her saying it, Elliot knows very well that she does not believe him, meaning that was strike two.

Thom is a little relieved to hear that Elliot has been lying. Violet knows a man's heart well. She knows that someone like Hawk who would risk his life to save his men on a dangerous cliff would never come all the way over here just to betray his own superior.

"I am going to give you another chance to answer that question."

"I am telling you the truth! He was going to kill General Thomas and make it look like you guys did it!"

"Uh, huh. And, how was he going to do that?" Even though Violet still does not believe him, she is curious to hear his answer.

"He didn't give us that many details."

"Convenient. And, what about your role in the hideout?" Violet asks knowing that this will be his third strike. He is obviously not going to admit being a double agent.

As expected, he answers, "What hideout?"

With that, Violet walks over to a silver cart in the corner. Elliot had noticed it before and had been wondering what it was for. On it were objects that looked like they belonged in a hospital rather than this place.

She slowly fills up a needle with a mysterious clear liquid and walks over to him. Is she going to kill him?

"Strike three."

She injects him in the neck.

"What the? What did you just shoot me with!?"

"Oh, it's my special three-part concoction. It's part truth serum, part paralyzing agent, and part toxin. In a minute, you will not be able to move your limbs, but will still be able to talk and move your eyes. You will also start feeling excruciating pain while telling me everything I asked you, truthfully this time. The best part is, you will have no idea what you told me when the serum wears off. Warned you not to lie, remember?"

In a panic, Elliot starts to convulse before he knocks his chair to the ground and lands on the floor.

"I will give you a minute to stop shaking." Violet says as she leans on the wall casually.

When he finally stops trembling, cold sweat starts to pour from his forehead as he starts to breathe harder.

"OK, I think you are ready. Why did you kill Hawk?"

"Mmmm, mmmm"

Elliot tries to shut his mouth as tightly as possible to stop himself from saying anything, but with each passing second, his efforts prove to be more and more futile.

"Hawk was a traitor."

At least one part of his previous answer was truthful.

"For whom?"

"He was helping the rebels."

Confused, Violet purses her lips. She would have known if Hawk was a double agent. Someone as high of a rank as himself would certainly be reported up to her. Since her serum has never failed before, there must be more to the story.

"How?"

"He was feeding intelligence to a woman named Lillian."

"Why her?"

"His original contact was her sister Sonya, but she was killed several years ago."

Having heard his mother's name, Max's hair stands on end. He is not sure if he wants to hear the rest of the interrogation. What if they go into grizzly details of her murder? He wouldn't be able to handle it. Seeing his friend shudder, Thom pats his shoulder. At least now they both know that Hawk is the John that Mrs. Sullivan mentioned in her journal.

"Why do the rebel leaders not know about this contact?"

"As a condition of his involvement, Hawk asked that he be anonymous and that there is no record of their discussion written anywhere."

"Because?"

"His previous contact was killed because someone found out about their liaison. He narrowly escaped when she was captured."

"Who killed her?"

"Lieutenant Marcel."

After hearing the name of his mother's killer, Max feels a rush of anger. Now, he knows who is truly at fault for her death. He sees red at the edges of his vision. He wants revenge for them, he can't stand it. Marcel has to die.

His imagination floods with images of his death. There are so many ways he can do it.

Shooting, drowning, poisoning, bludgeoning…

"How did he find out?"

Max snaps back to reality at her voice. He wants to hear the rest of the interrogation.

"After Sonya and her husband began their employment with the Legion, he received a top-secret mission from the Generalissimo to follow them."

This is the first time that either Thom or Max have heard of Victor's direct involvement in the Sullivans' deaths. Feeling deep remorse, Thom simply stares at the floor and cannot look in Max's direction. Max, on the other hand, is now adding to his anger. In addition to Marcel, he is going to have to take down Victor as well.

"Why Marcel and not Gillnet?"

"Marcel is the real head of intelligence. He handles all of the top-secret sensitive missions. Gillnet is just the front man who sorts through the daily inflow of dubious information."

"Why did they hire the Sullivans in the first place?"

"The Generalissimo knew about their connections with the Kerbasy tribe and hoped to get better intelligence on their whereabouts and movements."

Everything is starting to make sense now. Victor never cared for the Sullivans as friends. He was using them to get to the Desiderios. He apparently knows that El Diablo and the Warrior are both part of the same nomadic tribe.

After Trip's village was torched to the ground, the Kerbasy tribe began picking up orphans from other war torn villages.

Many of these lost children have become the top ranking officers in the Desiderios. Despite his bright disposition, Sunny is one of them. Even though he suffered a similar incident as Trip, he reacted to the situation in the opposite way. Instead of being dark and gloomy, he knows that he is lucky to be alive and wants to make the best of every day. Nevertheless, they are unified in a common goal, to take down Victor and the Legionnaires.

"What are the Legionnaires going to do with the Kerbasy?"

"Victor wants to use them as leverage against you."

"What has he found out so far?"

"He has their exact location and is lying in wait for the right time to attack."

For a second, Violet's heart starts to pound a little faster. This is first time that she has heard that her own family is being targeted. Even though she knows that they are well protected by some of her best men disguised as travelers, she is very much troubled by this news. Nevertheless, like the true professional that she is, she continues as if it does not faze her in the least bit.

"When is the *right* time?"

"I don't know. It was supposed to be sometime soon, but with young General Thomas's disappearance, there has been a change of plans."

"What will happen after you rescue General Thomas?"

"He will lead the attack on the rebel headquarters after Major Fouke leads another team to attack the Kerbasy tribe leaders and capture them as hostages."

Even though she does not show it outwardly, Violet is enraged that Victor can use innocent civilians in such a diabolic way in time of war.

"How is he going to be able to get in the headquarters?"

"I was going to show them the way."

"How did you know the way?"

"Someone showed it to me."

"Someone? Can you be more specific?"

"No, he is always dressed in black and covered from head to toe. He also disguises his voice so I cannot tell who it is."

Upon hearing the description of the man, Thom and Max instantly look at Trip, who looks as calm as ever. After all, he is the only man in the rebel camp who is always wearing black. Violet, on the other hand, continues without missing a beat.

"What else can you tell us about him? Height, weight?"

"He is tall and lean."

Thom and Max look at Trip again. Being well over 6 feet tall and weighing only about 180 pounds, it fits his description perfectly. This time, even Jordan is starting to look at the rebel leader with a suspicious eye. Again, El Diablo simply continues watching the interrogation. Of course, there are many tall and thin men who know how to get into the rebel headquarters.

"Why does he need to be in disguise?"

"He said it is better this way and is the condition for him showing me the way. In case I ever get captured, I cannot divulge his name."

"When did this conversation happen?"

"About a week ago."

That was about the same time that Thom went on his vacation. It's starting to sound a little too coincidental.

"How many of you traitors are in the hideout?"

"As far as I know, I am the only one."

"Have you told anyone else the location of our headquarters?"

"No."

"Why not?"

"Knowledge is power."

"Ah," Violet thinks to herself. "Self-promotion is a very powerful thing." If all of the Legionnaires keep vital information to themselves in hope of using it to their own advantage rather than to benefit the team as a whole, the Legionnaires have already lost before they even realize it. Satisfied with his answers, Violet shoots the antidote into Elliot's neck and puts him in lockdown.

Meanwhile, Trip hits Jordan in a pressure point on his neck, effectively paralyzing him for a moment before throwing him in a holding cell.

Having heard everything, it is pretty clear that Jordan is the man in black. Having a similar physique as El Diablo, he *is* the only man who knows the whereabouts of both the underground hideout and the rebel headquarters. Even though he has been trying to put the blame on someone else, Trip has always known who the real culprit is. He just needed someone to tell the story to Thom so the young general can see it for himself.

When Thom asks about the significance of the Kerbasy tribe, Violet tells him about her past. Even though he would never open his heart himself, she also told the young general about Trip's family and the image of Victor that has burned into his brain ever since the day he lost his childhood.

Once Thom and Max learn the truth about Victor's intentions, the Desiderios have gained their strongest allies. The general of their enemy is now firmly on their side along with his best friend. Being in the position of power both professionally and personally, Thom knows all of the secrets of the Legion. He has agreed to help Violet and Trip take down the Legionnaires with only one condition. His father is not to be harmed.

Staring into Thom's eyes emotionlessly, Trip is a little disturbed by this request. After what Victor did to his family, friends, and village, can he really just let him live? Does he have it in him to be so *merciful?* As far as he is concerned, a very public execution with a good old fashioned draw and quarter is the only way to go. Even if he does, will the other victims of his crimes like Sunny feel the same?

While Trip has wanted to watch Victor suffer for his crimes for many years, he understands Thom's position. No matter how evil he may be, he is still his father. Perhaps, it's a worse punishment to know that his only son has defected and turned his back against him than death itself.

To this end, Trip says, "OK, but I also have a condition."

"Name it."

"You have to be the one to capture him and lock him in his cell. I want to see the look in his eyes when you do it."

Shocked at the request, Thom pauses for a moment, but he, too, understands where Trip is coming from. After all, what is the one thing that is worse than death? The utter betrayal of a loved one.

Epilogue

At midnight, Thom leads the Desiderios into the Legion headquarters. Knowing the location of the security cameras and guards, they easily infiltrate enemy headquarters.

The Legionnaires aren't ready for an attack on their headquarters. The majority of them are sound asleep, prepping themselves to fight tomorrow. The entire rebellion force surges onto the headquarters, killing every soldier they can find, with anger in their veins.

By the time the sun rises above the horizon, most of the Legionnaires are dead or have deserted.

Fouke ran away in the beginning of the battle escaping his fate. He was a coward but he was lucky. None of the other high ranking officers made out as easily as he did.

Gillnet put up a courageous fight, but he was no match for the squads of fighters out for his blood. It wasn't long before his comrades fell and he was in the hands of the enemy.

And Marcel, he was a heavy sleeper, quite so heavy in fact, that he only woke up as the battle was already in its midst and many had died.

He went out of his room to fight like the brave soldier he was, but was ultimately captured as well as the fighting quelled down.

They vowed vengeance on their captors but alas, they did not have the chance. Both of them are to be executed at midday.

It took only two shots for the great leaders to fall from grace and into the ground.

*

Victor, however, merely sits in his office awaiting his fate. Once he hears that his son is leading the charge, he knows the end is near. As Thom storms in, Victor looks up to gaze into his eyes, eyes that were as cold as he had ever seen.

"Congratulations, son, you have finally won," he utters before the Desiderios drag him out of the headquarters. As promised, Thom personally locks his father in a rodent infested dungeon deep beneath the ground in total darkness with no hope of escape. That is where he is destined to live out the rest of his days.

Even though he is ashamed to be his father's son, he has to know why.

*

It takes a long while, but he finally summons the courage to go down and see him. When he confronts his father, Victor merely says, "I did it all for you."

With tears in his eyes, Thom walks out of the retched dungeon with heaviness in his heart but a hope for the future to be better. Max waits at the entrance for him and they leave together.

*

Violet and Trip are still in the rebel headquarters. They now have a lot of things to deal with, but it will be easier than everything they've done to make it up to this point.

"Trip! Where are you!" Violet roams the halls, searching for him. It doesn't take long until she reaches a window overlooking his garden. She watches as he crouches down, and with tenderness, cares for his flowers.

She walks away, leaving him to his thoughts.

*

He sees the fleeting shadow that is Violet, and not for the first time, is glad that she knows him so well. He wants to be alone.

Trip is caring for his flowers, but they are no ordinary flowers. They're Asphodel.

And for once, they seem to create a peace in his heart. So he stands up from them, and brushing off the dirt, climbs into his hammock and closes his eyes.

There's another day to come.

About the Author

Megan H. Lee is a college student in North Carolina. She started writing books in elementary school and has kept her passion for literature. The idea of the Balavan series started when she was in middle school, and years in the making have contributed to make the book. This is her first novel written in collaboration with her mother Sylvia S. Lee, who adds to the intrigue and suspense of the series with her love of history and imagination.

www.ingramcontent.com/pod-product-compliance
Lightning Source LLC
Chambersburg PA
CBHW030610130626
46552CB00017B/43